The most difficult qu

Dad looked me squarely in the eye. "What are the odds of succeeding in ballet?"

I couldn't answer him. An image of Madame Caroline appeared before my eyes and in my head I heard her saying, "There will always be someone who's a better dancer than you—"

"Does the Colorado Ballet have room for you? Or what about those companies in New York?"

"I know it's competitive—"

"I almost wish you never took up ballet," Dad said.

Tears sprang to my eyes. "How can you say that?"

"Because I was afraid this day would come." Dad raised his voice. "Even if you are good, even if you are the best, do you really think you have a chance to be treated fairly?"

I said nothing.

"How many black ballerinas can you name?"

I stirred my stew, watching a tear drop into it and disappear. But Dad said nothing else. He'd made his point.

"Lovers of this classic literary choreography will relish seeing this appealing young dancer in the starring role." —*BCCB*

OTHER PUFFIN BOOKS YOU MAY ENJOY

Blue Tights Rita Williams-Garcia

Big Star Fallin' Mama Hettie Jones

Lives of Our Own Lorri Hewett

Soulfire Lorri Hewett

A Time for Dancing Davida Wills Hurwin

LORRI HEWETT

dancer

PUFFIN BOOKS

Special thanks to Kabby Mitchell III
whose knowledge of the dance world was invaluable to me
in the writing of this book.

PUFFIN BOOKS
Published by the Penguin Group
Penguin Putnam Books for Young Readers,
345 Hudson Street, New York, New York 10014, U.S.A.
Penguin Books Ltd, 27 Wrights Lane, London W8 5TZ, England
Penguin Books Australia Ltd, Ringwood, Victoria, Australia
Penguin Books Canada Ltd, 10 Alcorn Avenue, Toronto, Ontario, Canada M4V 3B2
Penguin Books (N.Z.) Ltd, 182-190 Wairau Road, Auckland 10, New Zealand

Penguin Books Ltd, Registered Offices: Harmondsworth, Middlesex, England

First published in the United States of America by Dutton Children's Books,
a division of Penguin Putnam Books for Young Readers, 1999
Published by Puffin Books, a division of Penguin Putnam Books for Young Readers, 2000

10

THE LIBRARY OF CONGRESS HAS CATALOGED THE DUTTON EDITION AS FOLLOWS:
Hewett, Lorri.
Dancer / Lorri Hewett.—1st ed.
p. cm.
Summary: Sixteen-year-old Stephanie struggles to perfect her ballet dancing as her classes are complicated by the introduction of a new male dancer.
[1. Ballet dancing—Fiction. 2. Afro-Americans—Fiction.] I. Title.
PZ7.H4487Dan 1999 [Fic]—dc21 98-55501 CIP AC

Puffin Books ISBN 0-14-131085-5

Printed in the United States of America

for kevin gerard linder

dancer

one

The cast list was up, and my name wasn't at the top of it. There it was: THE SLEEPING BEAUTY in big block letters and underneath it—Princess Aurora: Anna Gritschuk. The words blurred over before they became clear again. This was supposed to be my year. Me, Stephanie Haynes, who's been taking ballet classes here at the South Metropolitan School of Ballet for ten years, since I was six. Last year I danced the Fairy Godmother in *Cinderella*. Not a bibbidi-bobbidi-boo grandmother like in the Disney cartoon, but an elegant queen in pink tulle and a silver crown. *When you're Sleeping Beauty* . . . that's how the talk went at the studio. Even when Anna Gritschuk showed up at the studio three weeks ago. I looked over my shoulder in class one day to see a girl about my height, with skin so white I could see blue veins in her forehead. She looked like a ballerina, more than anyone else I knew. After class she left quickly, without saying a word to anybody.

Okay, Anna was good—no, she was great, but I've been here longer. Scanning the casting sheet, I saw my name next to the Lilac Fairy. The next-best part, just like the Fairy Godmother last year. *She'll look more like Princess Aurora than you would.* It was my ugly voice, the voice that whispered to me whenever I felt most insecure. *Whoever heard of a black Princess Aurora?*

"Congratulations on being cast as Lilac Fairy." Madame Caroline, my teacher for the past two years, was behind me.

I didn't move, afraid I'd say something foolish.

"Stephanie?"

I faced my teacher, but I couldn't look at her so I kept my eyes on the floor. I sensed her disapproval.

"You seem disappointed."

My cheeks burned. Luckily, no one was in the lobby to see us. In Studio 1, a teacher's voice rang "And one and two . . ." over the familiar tinkle of a piano. In the early afternoon, the ballet school becomes Munchkinland, full of the little girls who keep the studio in business so that Madame Caroline can train us advanced dancers.

"Your silence tells me I'm correct." Madame Caroline didn't sound particularly sympathetic to me. But then again, I could never really tell what she thought about anything. I looked up at her, looked up because she's five feet ten. Too tall, really, for a ballet dancer, but she was a soloist with the Colorado Ballet for many years. Her brown hair, threaded with silver, was pulled back into a severe bun. I always feel insignificant under her gaze, like I don't quite add up somehow.

"I know you don't want to hear this," she continued in her

usual inexpressive voice, "but Anna's a better dancer than you are."

"But she's only been here three weeks!" I blurted before I could stop myself.

"Roles aren't handed out based on seniority. Lilac Fairy is a wonderful part, and you'll do well in it."

I couldn't speak.

"I know you're disappointed, but consider this a lesson." Madame Caroline looked me in the eye. "There will always be someone who's a better dancer than you are. Now, how are you going to deal with that?"

She left me standing there. I swallowed my tears and trudged to the dressing room. Class didn't start until four, and at three forty-five, I was the only girl from the advanced class there. I took off my school uniform, folding the skirt and sweater neatly and laying them on a bench. My tights, formerly pink, were faded colorless from so many washings. My leotard, formerly black, was a dingy gray, and my ballet slippers were scuffed and worn. As I dressed for class, Madame Caroline's words rang in my ears. She was right; there always would be dancers who were better than me. So why do I bother? Why drag myself to the studio six days a week if there's always going to be someone who'll waltz in and be a better dancer? Sinking onto the bench, I let my head drop forward into my hands.

"Stephanie? Are you okay?"

I looked up as the Weaver twins sat down on either side of me: Camilla, who smelled of smoke and whose straight blond hair was pulled over one shoulder, and Ursula, quiet and sweet, who put an arm around my shoulder.

I rubbed my face. "I'm fine."

"You should've been Princess Aurora," Ursula said.

"How do we know if this girl's even gonna show up for rehearsals?" Camilla said, then coughed. "Maybe she'll start taking classes downtown."

"What would be the point?" I said. Our school was affiliated with the Colorado Ballet—we performed in their *Nutcracker* at Christmastime—and it was just as easy, or I should say just as difficult, to get into the Colorado Ballet from our school as it was from their own academy.

"Still, it's not fair," Camilla said.

I felt guilty—I was so wrapped up in myself I hadn't even bothered to check the rest of the cast list. "And what about you guys? What parts did you get?"

"I'm Red Riding Hood." Ursula looked away, her arm falling from my shoulder. I could sense her disappointment. Red Riding Hood's a small role—she's one of the guests in the final wedding scene.

"I'm some fairy or another, I forget." Camilla rummaged through a grubby backpack, tossing wads of lamb's wool and dirty leotards onto the floor.

"Fairy of the Golden Vine," Ursula said bitingly. "It's a great part."

Camilla shrugged, apparently finding what she was looking for, a crumpled pack of cigarettes. "I'm going outside for a smoke." She gathered her hair in her hands and shook it out, so that it fell like a shimmering golden curtain around her shoulders. In her ripped jeans and black tank top, she looked more like a biker girl than a ballet dancer. Well, if you didn't look at her turned-out feet—the "duck walk" we all have from rotating our hips so much.

"She should just quit," Ursula said when Camilla left the room. "It's not like she really cares about ballet."

I didn't answer, and Ursula changed into her leotard and tights.

Every ballet dancer must have turnout—so that when standing in first position, heels touching, the feet create a straight 180-degree line on the floor. A lot of people, especially those with bad teachers, make the mistake of wrenching their knees and ankles to the side to make their feet turn out. Turnout comes from the rotation of the legs in the hip sockets, and if you don't have it, you don't have it. My turnout isn't perfect. Poor Ursula has hardly any turnout at all. It's hard to believe Ursula and Camilla are twins, even though they say fraternal twins aren't any more related than any set of siblings—Camilla's so willowy, with her long legs and corn-silk hair, and Ursula's short and compact and keeps her blond hair cut in a short bob because it's too wiry to hold any other style.

Others from our class filed in, and the dressing room was soon crowded with girls changing clothes, pinning up hair, and, of course, talking about *Sleeping Beauty.* Several girls glanced in my direction, probably as surprised as I was that I wasn't going to be Princess Aurora. But did it really matter? How many ballet schools were in this city, or even in this country, filled with girls who dance every day, who work hard, who dream of joining a company? There are girls my age, sixteen, who are already in the New York City Ballet, the American Ballet Theatre, and here I am at a suburban school. Can I even compete at all? Am I foolish for thinking that I could? My ugly voice whispered, *If you're not the best here, how can you be the best anywhere?*

Anna Gritschuk walked in five minutes before class would begin, her hair in two scraggly white-blond braids. She ignored the chattering girls around her, changing in silence. I watched her brush out her hair with her fingers and gather it into a ponytail behind her head. My hair was already up—I wear it in a bun to school so I don't have to fuss with it. For the past few years I've been taking good care of my hair, growing it out so that it's long enough to wear up. Anna didn't look particularly proud or excited to have been cast in the lead of *Sleeping Beauty*. She looked like she always did: aloof.

In the studio I took my normal place at the barre, standing in profile to the mirror. We all have a love-hate relationship with mirrors. We joke around about skinny mirrors and fat mirrors, but, in truth, the mirror simply shows everything. It's made me smile and made me gnash my teeth in frustration.

A tall black woman entered the room as Madame Caroline was giving instructions to the accompanist. She walked like a queen, her head held high. She wore a silky purple turban and a matching purple dress that was so long it skimmed the floor as she walked. Heavy gold jewelry glittered at her throat and on her fingers.

"Who's the fortune-teller?" Camilla whispered from behind me, but I didn't say anything. The woman sat on a folding chair at the front of the room and began to survey each dancer. I felt myself pulling up taller as Madame Caroline called the class to attention. She didn't introduce the woman. She never introduces guests. Maybe she thinks we'll work harder that way, but we can usually tell if a guest is important—that is, if he or she knows anything about ballet.

I could feel the stranger's eyes on me as I worked at the barre, concentrating hard on each exercise. From the corner of my eye I could see her watching my feet. I was lucky to have been born with nicely arched feet. Camilla, whose legs can extend to the sky, has feet that barely arch at all. As we worked,

Madame Caroline went around the room making corrections: manipulating a hand, straightening a leg. Ballet is an art about perfection. Or, better yet, working toward perfection.

During the center-floor *adagio,* certainly not my best exercise, the woman stared at Anna, who lifted her leg high to the front and rotated it to the side without a wobble. I couldn't help but watch, too. Anna was really good; there was no point in denying it.

But then came my favorite exercise, *pirouettes.* I'm what's called a natural turner. I don't think about it. I just place my feet, *plié,* and turn. The combination was easy today. I did doubles, triples, even a quadruple—four rotations on one leg, getting applause from the class and a raised eyebrow from our visitor.

The last exercise is the one everyone loves—*grand allegro.* We drill and train for an hour and twenty-five minutes in order to feel like we're really dancing the last five minutes of class. Even Ursula smiles during the waltzy turns, the giant leaps.

At five-thirty, we had a ten-minute break to change shoes for pointe class. I decided to be a good sport and congratulate Anna.

She sat bent over on a bench, carefully tying the ribbons of her pointe shoes. Her arms were spindly—a millimeter less flesh and she would look emaciated. Up close she was imposing-looking more than anything else: a severe face with a small upturned nose, eyelashes and eyebrows so blond they appeared colorless. But far away, on stage, I had to grudgingly admit, she would make a stunning Princess Aurora.

I cleared my throat. "I just wanted to say congratulations—"

She looked up when I spoke, seemingly surprised.

"—on being cast as Princess Aurora. You'll do a good job." I didn't sound as sincere as I meant to.

"Thank you." The surprised look never left her face.

Well, I had said all I had to say. Anna went into the studio. Through the doorway I could see her standing on pointe in the rosin box. But the chair where our guest had been sitting was now empty. Curious, I peered out of the dressing room into the lobby.

There she stood, her arms crossed, like she was waiting for someone. She was taller than any older woman I had ever seen, and she was old, even though her face wasn't that wrinkled and her hair was hidden under her turban. Her eyes told me that she had lived for many years. Her skin was deep black. Her dress looked like it was made of silk or some other fine fabric. Her clothes did seem costumish, but I wouldn't say that she looked like a fortune-teller. The heavy chain around her neck and the chunky rings on her fingers looked, at least to my untrained eyes, like real gold. Her posture was erect, her back broomstick straight. Her toes pointed outward as she stood, which made me think she'd spent many years turning out her hips. She looked more like an ex-dancer than anyone I had ever seen. Or an ex-performer of some kind. She was just too flamboyant not to be.

She looked toward the dressing room and, seeing me, smiled a little. "Stephanie."

I stood in the doorway, wondering how she knew my name.

Her smile broadened. "Come out, don't be shy." Her voice was as magisterial as her appearance.

I stepped into the lobby.

"Your dance teacher told me your name. And that you take class six days a week. Oh heavens, I haven't introduced myself.

My name is Wilhemina Price." She seemed to glide across the floor as she came to shake my hand. Up close I could smell her perfume, spicy and exotic.

"Hello," I said.

"I have a nephew about your age. I'm bringing him to class tomorrow."

"He's a dancer?"

"He's quite good. I've been teaching him myself, but he needs to start taking a class. Your teacher tells me she gives a partnering class tomorrow."

"Yes, every Wednesday."

"Good. I'd like it if you would be his partner tomorrow. It might make him more comfortable."

Because I was black? That seemed to be the most likely possibility. "Is he nervous?"

"I wouldn't say nervous. I think he's just not really certain what to expect."

"I'll be his partner then," I said. It wasn't really much of a favor—ballet schools are always short on men. We "import" ours from the Colorado Ballet—men who used to train at our school and are now junior members of the company.

Wilhemina Price looked me up and down, like she was studying me carefully. The music started for pointe class, but I didn't move.

"Um . . ." I wasn't quite sure how to address her. "Are you a ballet teacher?"

"I used to dance. A long time ago. Do you always work so hard in class, as hard as you did today?"

"I . . . try to. I want to be a dancer more than anything." I was surprised when I said that. I don't say it out loud very much. It's my own private dream.

"You should work on your *battements tendus,*" she said. "I'll see you tomorrow."

She glided up the stairs and out the front door and I stood where I was, openmouthed. *Battements tendus?* We do them as a warm-up. It's the second thing you learn in pee-wee ballet classes after *plié.* What did she mean by that? Was it some kind of insult?

I could hear Madame Caroline counting out a barre combination in the studio. Sighing, I went to join them.

two

During pointe class, I couldn't do anything right. Watching Anna do perfect triple *pirouettes* made me grit my teeth in frustration. Every now and then I'd point my foot in a *tendu* and look into the mirror. If I couldn't do a simple thing like a *tendu,* then maybe I couldn't do anything. That woman must've been laughing when I told her I wanted to be a dancer. Forget about it, I imagined her saying. You'll never make it.

I left the studio quickly, without talking to anybody.

Mom picked me up after class. It's on her way home from work. As usual, she asked me how class went as I slumped into the front seat of her battered Ford Tempo. I gave my usual answer: "Fine," which told her pretty much nothing. Sometimes when I say "fine" I mean "great, wonderful," and other times, like today, I mean "awful." But how can I say more than "fine" to either of my parents, who don't have much of a clue what I'm doing every day, or why? The car smelled faintly of dog food. Mom works at Ralston Purina in an ugly, industrialized part of Denver. She's a secretary in the office, but the smell of the factory infuses everything.

Mom drove through the neighborhood in silence. My ballet school is in a really nice part of town, Cherry Hills Village, which I hear is one of the richest suburbs in America. My school, Lakeview Country Day, is in Cherry Hills, too. I attend only because my father works there and I have a scholarship.

Our neighborhood is just fifteen minutes from the studio: small, squarish houses with tiny front lawns. Not poor, but not the kind of picket-fence neighborhood most people associate with Middle America. People in my neighborhood work hard for what they have. They work in places like the post office and the grocery store. They fix traffic lights and leaky faucets.

Dad was making dinner when I came in; stew, by the smell of it. "Dinner's almost ready," he called from the kitchen as Mom trudged upstairs to take a shower. Feeling sticky and gross from two ballet classes, I went to my bathroom down in the basement to do the same.

Three large envelopes lay on my pillow, all of them torn open. I seethed at that, because they were all addressed to me. But it was college stuff, which I guess Dad feels is his business as well as mine. I dumped out the contents of the envelopes on my bed, and thick, glossy catalogs fell onto my bedspread. Northwestern, Duke, Amherst. Each one came with an official letter. I picked up one and skimmed it. "Dear Stephanie: We at Northwestern were impressed with your PSAT scores and would like to invite you to apply. . . ." I stuck the letter into the envelope and tossed all three catalogs into the bottom drawer of my desk. Then I peeled off my sweaty leotard and tights, leaving them on the floor as I went in to shower. The rush of hot water felt good on my aching muscles. I wiggled my toes on the slippery tile, shutting my eyes as steam rose all around me. It would be nice to stay in the warm, moist cocoon of the shower, instead of going upstairs to face dinner with my parents. But I shut off the water and reached for a towel, drying myself briskly before the cool air from my bedroom seeped in.

I wrapped a robe around myself and went upstairs, where Mom and Dad were already seated at the table, waiting for me. Mom was dressed in a bathrobe like me, with enormous, round glasses perched on her nose. I don't know why she wears glasses like that. They make her look frumpy, and Mom isn't even forty yet. It's almost as if she's given up, allowing middle age to take over when she could look so good without a whole lot of effort.

"Did you read your mail yet?" Dad asked as I joined them at the table.

"I saw it," I mumbled. Mom ladled me a bowl full of stew and set it before me. "That's too much!"

"You've been dancing for three hours." Mom placed two corn muffins on my plate. I put one of them back, but said nothing else about it.

"Northwestern, Duke, Amherst," Dad said.

"It looks like you saw them, too."

Either Dad didn't get my point or he chose to ignore it. "Those are all wonderful schools. I'll bet you'll start hearing from the Ivy League soon."

I stirred my stew, which looked starchy and heavy. If I ate it all, I'd never be able to sleep tonight. "They just sent me catalogs."

"They wouldn't be sending you catalogs if they weren't

interested in you," Dad said. "Northwestern looks like it has a Fine Arts program, so you could still take ballet lessons—"

"That sounds wonderful," Mom echoed.

I put a spoonful of stew in my mouth so I wouldn't have to answer.

Dad went on. "College time will be here before you know it."

"Dad—" I really didn't want to be having this conversation.

"Stephanie." Dad was starting to look impatient. He folded his thick hands on the table, and his forehead creased. "Look at me and your mother."

"What?" I was already looking at him. I glanced at Mom, who was looking at Dad as well, as if she was wondering what he was going to say.

"Look at us," Dad said again, without raising his voice. So I looked. Dad really isn't heavyset, even though he has a large stomach. His eyes were bloodshot from fatigue, his hairline receding and tinged with gray.

"What?" I said again.

"You don't understand how hard it is to succeed without a college degree," Dad said. "I didn't have the opportunities you have, to go to a wonderful school like you do. There's so much you can do if . . ." He paused.

"If I stop dancing, you mean," I said faintly.

"No one said anything about stopping," Dad said. "I know you love to dance—"

"No, you don't know!" I stood up, looking from Dad to Mom. "Ballet is my life!"

"Stephanie," Mom said.

I sat down in my seat, breathing deeply.

"You could do absolutely anything you want to do," Dad said. "You could be your own boss without punching a time clock like your mother and me. We just want the best for you."

Want the best for me. I could hear what they meant, behind the code. It was so obvious. "I do everything you ask me to do," I said, careful to keep my voice steady. "I get good grades, I work hard at school. I have a scholarship to pay for my ballet lessons."

"I know, and I'm proud of you," Dad said. "But are you being entirely realistic?"

"You just said I could do anything I wanted to do!" I exclaimed. "But that doesn't include ballet, does it?"

"Maybe I should ask you that question." Dad looked me squarely in the eye. "What are the odds of succeeding in ballet?"

I couldn't answer him. An image of Madame Caroline appeared before my eyes and in my head I heard her saying, "There will always be someone who's a better dancer than you—"

"Does the Colorado Ballet have room for you? Or what about those ballet companies in New York?"

"I know it's competitive—"

"I almost wish you never took up ballet," Dad said.

Tears sprang to my eyes. "How can you say that?"

"Because I was afraid that this day would come." Dad raised his voice. "Even if you are good, even if you are the best, do you really think you have a chance to be treated fairly?"

I said nothing.

"How many black ballerinas can you name?"

I stirred my stew, watching a tear drop into it and disappear. But Dad said nothing else. He'd made his point.

"I forgot to ask," Mom said after a few moments of uncomfortable silence. "When do you find out if you got the lead part in the recital?"

I swallowed hard but didn't look up. "It's not a recital." My voice was shaky when I spoke. "Recitals are for little kids. It's a performance."

"Well, then, when do you find out if—"

"I didn't get it, okay!" I stood up now and pushed out my chair. I couldn't stand to watch my father gloat over this news, to hear him say, "I told you so." So I fled the table and went downstairs to my room, slamming the door behind me. Falling onto my bed, I began to sob. I curled myself up into a ball, wishing I could retreat into a shell like a snail. Hot tears wetted my bathrobe, and my chin shook. It was everything weighing down on me: seeing Anna Gritschuk's name next to Princess Aurora on the cast list; Madame Caroline and her snide remark; that lady telling me my *tendus* were bad; and now my parents telling me I can never make it, that my dreams to be a ballet dancer are just that, silly dreams.

Turning onto my side, I stared at the one ballet poster I have in my room: three nameless dancers in practice clothes leaping in the air. It's like flying, the sense I have when I'm really dancing, that moment when I'm suspended in the air. The throbbing ache in my legs made my eyes smart even more. Why do I work so hard for that one moment of flight? It seems silly when I think about it, arranging my whole life around a few moments of pure joy. I turned away from the poster, miserable.

I heard a soft knock on my door. When I didn't answer it, the door opened and my mother came into the room. "Stephanie—"

I sat up quickly and wiped my eyes. "I'm fine."

She came to sit on the edge of my bed. "I'm sorry you didn't get the lead."

I shrugged. "The new girl got it."

"New girl? That doesn't seem fair."

"Well, it is." I tried to sound as noncommittal as possible. "She's a better dancer than me. Besides, I got cast as the Lilac Fairy. It's the next-best part. I'll be dancing in every scene."

"It sounds wonderful." Mom sounded like she wanted me to tell her more about it, but I was too tired and upset to say much.

"I have homework to do."

Mom got up and moved slowly toward the doorway, but I wanted her to leave. "I'll be upstairs—"

"Good night."

Mom closed the door behind her, and I turned to stare at my ballet poster again. Maybe it was just an impossible dream, like winning the lottery. But the idea of not dancing scares me. I just don't know what else I'd want to do.

three

Third period has to be the worst hour of my school day. It's a study hall, right before lunch, and all I can think about is how to make the fifty minutes go by quickly until lunchtime. You're allowed to talk as long as you whisper. So that's what most of the students do, sit around whispering in small groups. A few of us study. Or, at least, pretend to.

I always get a sick feeling in my stomach before going to study hall. It's exactly the same feeling I get when I'm riding to school with Dad in the morning, like I'm about to crash a country club party where I don't belong. Sure, I'm dressed like everyone else. All the girls at Lakeview wear navy-blue skirts, white blouses, and navy cardigans with the Lakeview crest emblazoned over the left pocket. But I feel like a complete outsider.

I had some trigonometry homework, but all the sine and cosine curves swam on the page as I sat by myself near the back of the room, trying my best to be invisible. My ears picked up the conversation near me, as much as I tried to shut it out. Kelly Corbell, Lisa Brown, Gillian Sporer, three of the most popular girls at school, were talking about some college guy Lisa met at a party last week.

"And then we're going downtown for a carriage ride," Lisa was saying. "The problem is, the show won't get out before eleven, and he wants to take the carriage ride after. I have to figure out a way to stay out past curfew. I don't want to look like a little kid or something."

"Say you're spending the night at my house," Gillian suggested.

"Won't work. My mom plays bridge with your mom," Lisa said.

Some people, I think, are just born having everything going for them. I've been attending school with Kelly and Lisa since third grade. Gillian's new; she just moved here from Atlanta in the fall. She's the only other black girl in my grade. But as soon as she arrived, she was sucked into Lisa and Kelly's clique. All three of them wear their hair the same way: long and permed, so that it cascades down their backs in curls. Lisa's the prettiest of the three, I think, with hair that looks blond sometimes and brown sometimes, highlighted so it seems as if she has a perpetual spotlight shining on her. Kelly used to be in my ballet class, but she quit two years ago.

I was curious about Gillian, but she had a snobby, standoffish look just like her new friends. She had long jet-black hair, and skin the color of caramel. She drives a pale gold Mercedes convertible that even in a parking lot full of expensive cars everyone notices.

"Do you want to stay out late, or stay out all night?" Kelly asked, giggling.

"I have an idea," Gillian said, and they all bowed their heads together. Gillian glanced my way, and I looked down at my homework. But from the corner of my eye, I saw all three of them coming toward me.

"Hey, Stephanie," Gillian said as they surrounded me. The scents of musky perfume, hairspray, and cinnamon chewing gum mingled together, overpowering me.

"We were thinking . . ." Kelly played with a gold chain around her neck (a gift from her boyfriend, I heard her exclaim after Christmas). "What are you doing this weekend? Saturday night?"

I hesitated, then said, "I haven't made plans yet."

"What if you had a slumber party at your house?"

"My house?" My cheeks warmed. None of them had ever been to my house. Hardly anyone I know has been to my house.

"It wouldn't be a real slumber party." Gillian looked impatient, as if she had important things to do and I was wasting her time. "Could we just say we're having a slumber party at your house?"

"Um . . ." I didn't know what to say.

"You see, I have a date with this guy, Michael. He's a freshman at DU, and I don't want to worry about making curfew." Lisa sounded even more impatient than Gillian. "You'll help us out, won't you?"

"What do I have to do?" My voice was a low mumble and my heart pounded fiercely. Why was I so nervous all of a sudden?

"Nothing. If my mom calls to find out details, you answer the phone and make something up," Lisa said.

"What if your mom wants to speak to my mom?"

Lisa shrugged. "Say she's not home. It's no big deal, really." She looked at me like she expected me to say yes.

"I have ballet after school. I don't get home until after seven—"

"I'll tell my mom to call after seven, then." Lisa tapped her fingers on the desk. Gillian and Kelly looked expectant as well. My lips tightened as my chest continued to pound. What was I supposed to say?

I sighed. "Okay—"

"Great! You're the best," Kelly said. Lisa immediately left and went to her seat, where she pulled a compact from her purse. But Kelly and Gillian stayed where they were. I looked from one to the other, suspicious.

"How's ballet going, anyway?" Kelly asked. She was looking at me in a way that told me she wasn't seeing me at all, just looking in my general direction.

"Fine . . ." My voice was faint, but inside I was seething. Why did I freeze up around them, turn to stone?

"It was too much for me," Kelly said. "All those classes every day. I mean, how're you supposed to have a life?"

"I used to take ballet." Gillian pulled her heavy black hair over one shoulder. "I was thinking about starting up again here. Where do you take?"

"South Metro," Kelly cut in. "We used to be in the same class. It's pretty hard-core. And Madame Georgina used to say things like, 'Too many pizzas, girls? Too many cookies?' " She affected an English accent. "Old bat."

I felt my face burning again.

"Half the girls in our class were anorexic," Kelly went on.

That wasn't true at all. Only one girl had an eating disorder and that was Ursula Weaver, but I think she would have had an eating disorder whether she was in ballet or not. And she's been through counseling.

"What happened to that one girl?" Kelly asked.

"Ursula." My voice was cold with my anger. "She's still dancing."

"Really?" Kelly laughed. "It's not like she was any good. Not like her sister, anyway."

My jaw clenched.

"That might be too much for me, then," Gillian said.

In the moment of silence that followed, Kelly and Gillian glanced at each other, then Kelly said a quick "See ya," and they went back over to where Lisa was sitting. I guess they didn't have anything else to say to me. The way the three of them sat together, whispering conspiratorially, flipping their hair, twisting their necklaces, they looked almost staged somehow, as if they were used to people watching them, envying them. And now I, the chump, was part of their sneaking-out duplicity.

Thankfully, the bell rang a few minutes later. I went to my locker to get my lunch. To get to the cafeteria, you exit the Upper School wing and go down a huge staircase to a lobby with an incredible crystal chandelier hanging above it. You go down a long hallway lined with portraits of various donors and trustees, all looking down imperiously, to a large, airy room with a back wall made entirely of windows, overlooking a golf course.

Bridget Alfonso came to sit with me, carrying two yogurts, peach for me, strawberry for her. Bridget's only fourteen, but we've been eating lunch together ever since she started taking Advanced Ballet with me this year. We both had the same thing for lunch: small tuna sandwiches on wheat bread, an apple, bottled water, yogurt.

"I'm so sore from yesterday's class," Bridget said as she sat down. Her hair was up in a bun like mine.

"Me, too." I opened my yogurt. "A new guy's coming to partnering class today."

"Who?"

"Remember the woman who watched our class yesterday?"

"Who is she?"

"I'm not sure, but she has a nephew or something and she's been teaching him ballet. She asked me to work with him in partnering class."

"I'll bet Madame Caroline shanghais him into *Sleeping Beauty,*" Bridget said, giggling. "If he has two legs, that is."

I laughed, too. There were only three guys our studio could count on for sure, but there were five Fairies who needed partners, not to mention a Prince for Sleeping Beauty.

"I'm so excited about *Sleeping Beauty*!" Bridget said. "I've never done partnering on stage before."

"Me neither."

She frowned. "I think it's awful you didn't get the lead. I mean, what does anyone know about that new girl, anyway?"

I didn't answer.

Bridget sniffed. "I think she's stuck-up!"

I shrugged. It was hard to tell with Anna. She moved in a confident way, like she knew she was a good dancer. But she didn't really seem arrogant to me. She always stood at the back of the room during class, unless Madame Caroline brought her to the front.

We fell silent as we ate lunch. In my opinion, Bridget looked even more stuck-up than Anna: an upturned nose, eyebrows she had razored into thin lines like a 1940s movie star, strawberry-blond hair that was always in a bun. She's not even five feet tall. She would look ten years old if it weren't for those razored eyebrows. She was cast as the Bluebird in *Sleeping Beauty* because of her quick and nimble feet.

She tore small pieces from her sandwich and chewed them slowly. She ate a spoonful of yogurt for every three bites of her sandwich. Watching Ursula deal with bulimia a few years ago made me really vigilant when it comes to food. And an early warning sign of disordered eating is strange eating habits. But Bridget was eating, at least.

After lunch, I hurried up the stairs and down the hallway to my locker. If I moved fast enough, I could miss seeing my father in the hallway. But as I turned a corner, I saw him in his blue work shirt. He was coming my way, so I couldn't avoid him. The hall was choked with rowdy kids making noise and pushing one another, even as teachers warned them from doorways to be orderly. Seventh through twelfth grades are housed together at Lakeview, which is why passing period is so disorderly. I could feel the perspiration breaking out on my forehead and the tension in my shoulders as I folded my arms across my chest.

No one paid attention to Dad. Pulling a waist-high gray trash basin on wheels, he picked his way through the crowd of blue skirts and blue slacks, students with Gucci watches and seventy-five-dollar haircuts, who drove cars that cost more than

Dad's annual salary. Dad looked pleasant enough; he always does. Yet I couldn't help but feel the shame creeping up my neck as we met eyes.

"Hi, Stephanie," he said as we passed each other. He smiled at me.

"Hi, Dad," I whispered. And it was done. I was past him, and we were moving in opposite directions. I took a deep breath and exhaled slowly, feeling like a jerk and feeling sad at the same time.

four

Bridget's mother picks us up from school on Mondays, Wednesdays, and Fridays to take us to ballet. The other days I walk because Bridget has math tutoring after school. The plush interior of Mrs. Alfonso's burgundy Lexus smelled like expensive perfume. Mrs. Alfonso is a buyer for Neiman Marcus, and she's always beautifully dressed, her cloud of frosted blond hair perfect to the strand.

"I heard you didn't get Sleeping Beauty," she said as I buckled myself into the backseat.

I was getting sick of the sympathy. "I got cast as the Lilac Fairy."

"Well, I think you were unfairly passed over. Did your mother call the studio?"

"No—"

"Your mother should call," Mrs. Alfonso said firmly. "Your teacher probably didn't want a black Sleeping Beauty."

I winced at that, but Mrs. Alfonso went on, oblivious. "I can't think of any other reason why you weren't cast. I think it's just awful!"

I could feel myself tensing up as I stared out the window. I'd never let my mom call the studio even if she wanted to. It would just make me look like a sore loser. Besides, Madame Caroline had already told me to my face why I wasn't cast.

"Thanks for the ride," I mumbled when she dropped us off.

Going down the stairs to the lobby, I saw Wilhemina Price sitting on a couch. She wore the same gold turban from yesterday, with a deep red floor-length gown and the same chunky gold jewelry. Next to her sat a sullen-looking boy. Or slumped is a better word. He wore a white tank top and baggy gray sweatpants, his legs splayed forward on the ground. From the length of his legs, I'd say he was at least six feet tall. He was the same deep brown shade as his aunt, great aunt, by the looks of it. He had a thin mustache. When he saw me, I watched his eyes trace me up and down, slowly. I felt self-conscious; after all, I was still wearing my stupid school uniform.

"Stephanie." Wilhemina Price stood up. "I want you to meet my nephew Vance. Vance, this is Stephanie."

He sort of nodded at me but didn't stand up. So I sort of nodded back.

"So you're a dancer." My voice wavered a little.

He gave a quick shrug as an answer, then looked at something behind me. I turned around and saw two of the guys who take Wednesday class with us coming down the stairs.

"Here come the queers." He stood up and did an awkward

pirouette on the tips of his toes. He didn't have the greatest posture in the world. "I'm here to be a ballerina," he said in falsetto. His aunt frowned, as if she disapproved.

I wasn't going to dignify that with a response, so I went to the dressing room.

Ursula and Camilla were already there, changing for class.

"Who's that guy in the lobby?" Camilla jerked her head toward the door. "He's hot!"

"Yeah, right!"

"That's the guy the fortune-teller woman told you about?"

"She's not a fortune-teller," I said. "She's a dance teacher. That guy doesn't look like a dancer to me."

Camilla elbowed me and laughed. "So you did check him out!"

"No, he just has a major attitude problem, that's all!"

She shrugged. "What guy doesn't have an attitude problem?"

Wilhemina Price was seated on a folding chair in the front of the studio as I took my place at the barre. I stretched out my legs, feeling awkward. According to her, I couldn't do *tendus*. But what did she know, anyway? Her nephew didn't look like he could do much of anything.

He stood in the doorway for a moment, surveying the room. To my annoyance, he sat on the floor next to me, shoulders hunched over. He didn't stretch at all. The three guys from the Colorado Ballet stretched out at the portable barre in the center of the studio. Vance watched them disdainfully. I personally love Wednesday classes. With the men here, it feels like a real company class. Anna took her place near the door. Stuck-up, Bridget called her. I watched Bridget stretching on the floor with a few of the younger girls not far from me. Even though Bridget and I eat lunch together every day, we rarely spend time in the studio together. We have our own groups of friends. Camilla rushed in right as Madame Caroline began the *plié* combination. Vance stayed where he was on the floor during the demonstration. Totally rude. He pulled himself to his feet as the music started.

I was in front of him so I couldn't see him do the combination on the first side. I studied myself in the mirror, working my turnout as hard as I could. When we turned around to the other side, I watched him, his back to me as he did the combination. He had looked sloppy before class, but now he stood with perfect posture. His turnout was much better than that of most men—most men don't have much natural rotation in their hips. But right after the combination, he slouched against the barre. The same thing happened all through barre. During each exercise, he stood erect, executing all the movements correctly, making no mistakes even on the tricky changes of direction in *frappé*. During the *développés,* his leg extension was higher than those of the men from the Colorado Ballet. Madame Caroline's eyes were drawn to him the whole time. She gave no corrections to anyone else; she just kept watching Vance. It was a little annoying. With each correction from Madame Caroline, he simply nodded. No attitude at all. I looked at his aunt in amazement. She had taught him all of this? But she wasn't watching him. She was practically the only one in the room not watching him. She was watching me.

In the center floor combinations, Vance continued to amaze everyone. He wobbled during *adagio* the way I do, but the height of his leg extensions was beautiful. He did triple and quadruple *pirouettes* with ease. During the *grand allegro,* he leaped so high he seemed to be hanging in the air. The men from Colorado Ballet looked impressed. Even Anna watched with raised eyebrows.

After class, Vance mopped his forehead and chest with a towel and slumped against the back wall. I went to the dressing room to put on my pointe shoes, and all I could hear was talk about Vance: "Where did he come from?" "Who taught him?" "Did you see his turnout?" "Did you see his feet?" "Did you see his extensions?"

After changing my shoes, I went back to the studio, which was humid with the stink of sweat. I stood on my toes in the rosin box so my feet wouldn't slip on the floor. The tips of my shoes were getting soft; I could feel my toes pressing against the floor. Madame Caroline was sitting next to Wilhemina Price, and they were talking. Vance was still slumped against the back wall. If I hadn't told his aunt I'd be his partner, I would have stayed as far away from him as possible. I made myself walk over to him and sit down, close enough to have a conversation but not close enough for him to think I was, well, interested.

"My aunt was talking about you last night," he said.

I spread my legs into middle splits. "She was?"

"Yeah. That's why she wants me to take class here."

I tried to keep my mouth from hanging open. "Because of me?"

"I guess she's been checking out studios all over Denver."

"She told me I have to work on my *tendus.*"

"She always says stuff like that."

"Well, I thought she meant I couldn't dance. She's your teacher?"

Vance shrugged.

"So you're serious about ballet?"

He pushed his hands out, like he was pushing the suggestion away. "I don't wanna be no sissy ballet dancer!"

"Dancers aren't sissies."

"Try telling that to someone where I come from."

I stretched forward, laying my chest on the floor. "Where do you come from?"

"The hood." He looked snide. "What about you? I saw your rich-girl school uniform."

I said nothing. What did he know, anyway?

We don't do barre in partnering class—the whole class takes place in center floor. There were only four guys (including Vance) to twelve girls, so we all had to share. For the past few weeks I've been working with Chris Martinez, who stood on the other side of the room with Bridget and some of the younger girls. He's really cute, I think. He has long black hair he pulls back into a ponytail, and a compact, muscular body. He's only twenty, but he's already married. The gossip in the dressing room is that his wife's going to have a baby.

"Can you imagine," said Camilla, who supplied the gossip, "having a baby on a corps de ballet salary? I hope his wife has a good job."

Madame Caroline clapped her hands, bringing class to order. She paired Camilla with Sidney, a tall blond with long, elegant legs. She had them demonstrate what looked to be a simple combination: Camilla *bourrée*ing toward Sidney, taking tiny, quick steps on the tips of her toes, into an *arabesque*. Sidney held her steady as she pitched forward in a *penchée*. We all admired Camilla's *penchée*, her legs arced into a six o'clock split.

"Stephanie and Anna, work with Vance," Madame Caroline said.

We looked at each other. Anna stood aside, like she wanted me to go first. As I took my *arabesque,* Vance grabbed my rib cage, his fingers digging into the bone.

"Lower," I whispered. He moved his hands to my waist, then tipped me forward to begin the *penchée.* But he didn't know how to hold me. I lost my balance and toppled to the floor.

He gave an "oh well" sort of shrug as I stood up. I was annoyed. He could have at least said he was sorry.

Anna went next. When she took her *arabesque,* she stepped too far and fell off pointe. It felt good to see her make mistakes like the rest of us.

We did supported *pirouettes* next, and Vance was a mess. He didn't know where to put his hands at all. He kept groping our waists, grabbing us at the wrong time. Vance looked embarrassed; Madame Caroline picked on him more than anybody. But he kept quiet and kept trying. At the end of class he left the room quickly, before anyone could say anything to him.

His aunt stood from her chair.

"Stephanie," she said, "thank you for working with Vance."

"It was no problem," I said, not adding that I would have sore ribs tomorrow because of him. "We need more guys around here, Mrs.—"

"Miss Winnie will do. That's what Vance calls me."

"Um, I've been working on my *tendus.*"

"Let me show you." With surprising agility for someone her age, and she had to be over sixty, she got down on her knees and instructed me to stand in fifth position. "It's like drawing a line with your whole foot, starting with your heel." She took my foot and pulled it along the floor until my toe was pointed squarely on the ground, my leg perfectly straight.

"That's where your *tendu* needs to be!" Miss Winnie said.

I looked in the mirror. My foot looked like it could be in a pointe shoe advertisement. I didn't know my feet could look like that. "I don't know if I could do that on my own."

"You will, in time. You have beautiful feet, but you must learn how to present them. Mr. Balanchine used to tell us, you have to present the foot to the floor."

"You knew George Balanchine?" I exclaimed. He was the greatest choreographer of the twentieth century. Saying you knew Balanchine was like saying you knew Picasso!

"I took classes at the School of American Ballet in the 1940s. Before he formed the New York City Ballet."

"Wow—" I didn't know what to say.

"You work hard, but you don't always work correctly." Miss Winnie stood up. "I teach Vance on Sundays at eleven-thirty, after church. You should come."

"I—I'd like that," I said. "But where?"

"My house." Her heels clicked on the floor as she walked across the studio to retrieve her purse. She took out a notebook and began writing down directions. She presented the sheet of paper to me with a flourish. "I'll expect you at eleven-thirty."

"I don't know," Dad said at dinner.

"Then I'll take the bus. I don't care, I'll find a way to get there!"

"Stephanie, what do you know about this woman?" Mom asked.

"I know she used to take classes with George Balanchine in

the 1940s. Do you know who he is? He started the New York City Ballet. He's one of the most important choreographers in history. And she has a nephew. She taught him herself, and he's fabulous."

Dad looked skeptical. "She's black?"

"Yes, she's black!"

"I didn't know black dancers could dance with white companies in the 1940s."

"She didn't say she was in the company, she said she took classes! And she can teach me!"

"Don't you take enough lessons at the studio?" Mom asked.

"I can't believe this!" I was shouting now. "Why are you being so impossible?"

"We just don't want you wearing yourself out," Dad said. "And stop shouting!"

I took deep breaths to control myself. "All I'm asking for is a ride. If you give me a ride on Sunday, then you can see for yourself that she's not a serial killer."

"All right, I'll take you," Mom said. "But how long is this class?"

I hadn't thought of that. "I don't know—"

"And what about payment," Mom asked. "Does she expect to get paid?"

"If she does, I'll pay for it out of my savings."

Mom and Dad looked at each other, but it was more as if they were giving in than anything else. I wished they could just be happy for me, be happy that someone was interested in me, thought I was worth teaching. But they just didn't seem to care.

After dinner, I got up from the table to go to my room, but

then I remembered what I'd told Gillian, Kelly, and Lisa. So I took my school bag to the den to be near the phone.

It rang at seven-thirty, and I answered it on the first ring.

"May I speak to Stephanie Haynes?" The voice sounded parentlike.

"This is she."

Dad came into the den with the newspaper, which made me nervous.

"This is Mary Brown. Lisa tells me you're having a birthday party Saturday night."

Birthday party? My birthday's in July! I swallowed. "Yeah."

"How nice of you to invite Lisa." The voice was chirpy and sweet. An image of a small woman with braces on her teeth came to mind, from a Back-to-School night. "What will you girls be doing?"

I twirled the phone cord around my finger. "I don't know, talking, mostly—"

"What time does it start?"

My palms were sweaty. "Um, six . . ." I said the first thing that came to mind.

"Wonderful. May I speak to your mother?"

"Um, she's not here." I looked over at Dad, whose head was in the paper. I prayed he wouldn't say anything. He looked up but said nothing.

"Okay then. Bye. And happy birthday."

"Thank you." I hung up the phone, breathing deeply. I wondered how Lisa did it, looked her mother in the face and lied. I felt like I was about to faint. Lisa's mom sounded really nice. I wonder how Lisa ended up so bitchy in comparison.

"Who was that?" Dad asked.

"Someone from school."

"Did I hear you making some plans?"

"No, not really. Some of us are going to meet after school tomorrow." I didn't sound very convincing. I left the room quickly, embarrassed and angry at the same time. I thought of Lisa and Kelly and Gillian and their stupid plans, how they had me lying for them. Well, I wouldn't ever do that again!

"You're the best," Lisa said to me the next day in study hall.

"Sure." I tried to sound as cold as possible, but I don't think Lisa noticed. She huddled up with Gillian and Kelly to make her weekend plans.

On Saturday night, when Lisa was out with her boyfriend and I was supposedly having a slumber party, I sat at home sewing ribbons on a new pair of pointe shoes and was in bed by ten o'clock.

five

Sunday mornings are usually pretty leisurely at my house because my parents sleep late. But I was up at eight. I read the whole Sunday newspaper as I waited for my parents to wake up. Then I got ready, putting on my best black leotard and pink tights, placing my new pointe shoes in my dance bag.

"Do you know where this woman lives?" Mom asked as we got into the car.

I showed her the directions. "It looks like Park Hill." Park Hill was in the northeast section of Denver, and we lived in the southeast section.

Mom drove into a neighborhood that looked a lot like our own—squarish houses made mostly of brick. Some ladies in pastel suits and hats stood on front porches.

"Must be on their way to church," Mom said. We didn't go to church very often. It's not that my parents have anything against church; they're usually just too tired on Sundays. So am I. It's my only day off from ballet. But I was excited to dance today, even though my body ached from a week's worth of hard classes.

We made a few wrong turns, circling one block a few times. We kept passing an old man sitting on his front porch in a bathrobe and slippers, smoking a pipe. He waved to us as we drove past him the third time. Mom smiled at that. I was starting to get an edgy, impatient feeling, but then Mom saw the turn she had missed up ahead.

"This should be it." Mom parked in front of a two-story house made of brown brick, one of the nicest-looking and largest houses on the block. All of the yards were yellow and dry because of the January cold, but I could tell that this yard was usually kept nice. The house had an old-fashioned wrought-iron lamppost in front and black shutters on the windows. There was no garage, just an empty carport next to the house.

"Why don't you come in with me and meet her," I said, and Mom followed me up the front walkway to the door.

Miss Winnie answered the door before I had a chance to lift the brass knocker. She wore a turban, royal blue this time, that matched a billowy blue pantsuit. Her face was made up dramatically, with lots of eye shadow and mascara. "Stephanie!" She stood aside to let us enter. Mom had a look on her face like she wasn't sure what to think.

"You must be Mrs. Haynes. Is it Mrs.?" Miss Winnie extended a graceful, manicured hand to Mom.

"Yes, it's Mrs.," Mom said in a low voice that sounded almost shy.

The house smelled like Miss Winnie's perfume: cinnamon

and cloves. The carpets were all white, as far as I could see. Miss Winnie ushered us into a brightly lit living room with white couches that gave off a rich, leathery smell. Two ceiling-high bookcases framed a brown brick fireplace, but neither held books. One held all kinds of pretty little objects, music boxes, from the look of it. There were gold carousels with miniature silver horses, a pink-tutued ballerina in *arabesque,* a tiny grand piano, cherubic angels with intertwined arms. I had an urge to wind them all up at once and listen to the tinkling music. The other bookcase held dolls—all kinds of dolls. Porcelain-faced Victorian dolls with blond curls and severe expressions, African dolls in golden robes, black-haired dolls in colorful kimonos.

"Can I get you some tea?" Miss Winnie asked. But before either Mom or I could answer, Miss Winnie disappeared into another room, and I soon heard a kettle boiling.

My eyes slowly swept over the room. On a wall opposite the fireplace hung four framed black-and-white photographs of a black woman in a light-colored chiffon dress and pointe shoes. In one picture, the woman's leg was sky-high in a plunging *arabesque* that looked like an arrow to heaven. In another, she stood in *sous-sous,* on the tips of her pointe shoes, her arms spread wide as if to announce her presence. The woman was young, but she had the unmistakable dramatic eyes and flamboyant flair of Miss Winnie.

"Can you believe it?" For some reason, I decided to whisper.

Mom was looking at the pictures, wide-eyed as I certainly was. "That was her?"

"Oh, look!" I went to an end table in the corner of the room, its surface lined with a row of pointe shoes. They all looked old and worn, the pink satin grayish and the ribbons dull. I was afraid to touch them; they looked brittle and fragile. Signatures in black ink were scrawled across the top of every pair, some of the signatures smudged, others faded with time. I could make out a few of them.

"Maria Tallchief, Margot Fonteyn, Allegra Kent—"

"Those are ballerinas?" Mom asked.

"Some of the most famous ballerinas ever!"

Miss Winnie entered, carrying a gleaming silver tea service. She set it carefully on the coffee table and poured tea into three tiny cups. Mom sat stiffly on one of the sofas, looking overwhelmed. Miss Winnie sat on the same sofa as Mom and crossed one leg over the other. The silky material of her suit draped around her. In her faded sweatpants and enormous glasses, Mom seemed haggard and worn next to Miss Winnie.

"Thank you," Mom said without touching her teacup. It was almost as if she was afraid to move.

Miss Winnie saw me studying the shoes. "I could tell you about each performance those shoes came from." She picked up her teacup and cradled it in the palm of her hand. "Do you see Virginia Johnson's shoe there?"

"Virginia Johnson." Mom glanced at me.

"She was the prima ballerina in the Dance Theatre of Harlem." I knew all about the Dance Theatre of Harlem, how it was started by Arthur Mitchell, the first black principal dancer in George Balanchine's New York City Ballet.

Miss Winnie nodded, smiling. She pointed to a creamy beige slipper, which stood out in the row of pale peach shoes. "That was from the first performance of *Creole Giselle.*" She raised her teacup to her lips and lowered it. To me, she looked wistful and a little bit sad. "The Dance Theatre of Harlem put on an all-black version of *Giselle,* changing the setting from a European village to Louisiana. I don't think I stopped crying during the entire ballet. I remember sitting there thinking, Now we've really made it."

I could hardly sit still. I wanted to get up and dance right then. Miss Winnie must have noticed my edginess because she set her teacup on her saucer and said, "Shall we begin?"

Mom got a tense, almost embarrassed look on her face, the look adults get when they wish they could squirm like kids. "Stephanie didn't tell us what these lessons would cost—"

Miss Winnie waved her hand in the air before Mom finished speaking. "It's my pleasure." She gave me a warm smile. "It's my pleasure to coach someone so talented."

I couldn't hide my smile. Miss Winnie thinks I'm talented. I repeated the words to myself over and over again.

Mom looked uneasy, as if she didn't know what to say. She hadn't yet stood up. It was almost like she didn't want to leave, even though I could tell she was anything but comfortable sitting in Miss Winnie's living room.

"We won't be longer than an hour today," Miss Winnie said. "I want us to work on some fundamentals."

That uncertain look didn't leave Mom's face as she turned to me. "You'll be all right?"

I nodded emphatically, picking up my dance bag off the floor. Why don't you just go, I wanted to say. I stood up, impatient to get to work.

Mom nodded and stood up as well. "I'll be back in an hour."

"Okay. Bye." My impatience showed in my voice. *She should leave, already.* It was my ugly voice, coming from a tiny corner of my mind. *Not like she belongs here, anyway.* Turning my attention to Miss Winnie, I tried to shoo the thought away.

"This way." Miss Winnie led me through a dining room and down a narrow hallway. "I turned the den into a studio."

"So you were a dancer?"

Miss Winnie nodded as she led me into an airy, sunlit room that smelled faintly of pine. An eastern wall had been knocked out and replaced with windows, which flooded the studio with sunlight. Another wall had a barre attached to it and opposite it, a wall of mirrors. "I took class at the School of American Ballet . . . when I could."

"Were you in a company?" I took off my shirt and jeans and lay them in a neat pile in the corner of the studio. I wore my leotards and tights underneath.

"I spent a year in the New York Negro Ballet and I danced in Europe for several years. But there will be time for stories later." Miss Winnie gave me a long, scrutinizing look. "How much do you weigh?"

My shoulders stiffened. I thought of Madame Caroline's acidic comments in class sometimes. Watch the junk food, girls, she would say, usually looking at one girl in particular. I remembered Madame Georgina, my teacher before Madame Caroline, and her "too many pizzas?" comments, usually directed at Ursula. And I remembered Ursula's lips trembling, her ears red with embarrassment. What would Miss Winnie say if I told her what I weighed? I wasn't heavy at all; in fact, the mirror showed me I was thin. It was just that my weight *sounded* like a lot, especially next to someone like Bridget, who's built like a little boy and weighs ninety pounds.

"I think you could lose a few pounds," Miss Winnie said.

I was practically shaking. "How many?"

"Two or three. No more than three."

I was a little relieved, even though my self-consciousness burned my face. "I guess I'm not a stick figure. . . ." I meant it as a joke, but it sounded more like an apology. After watching Ursula struggle with bulimia, I knew all about eating disorders and how destructive they were. But still, sometimes I stood at the barre in class, looking at Bridget or looking at Anna, and my ugly voice, out of my control, would whisper, *You'd be a better dancer if you looked like her.*

"No one said anything about stick figures, dear," Miss Winnie said. "Arthur Mitchell would tell you the same thing. Two pounds. You should be able to do that safely. Your body is your instrument, and you must treat it well. Do you eat well? Lots of fruits and vegetables?"

I nodded. I don't like vegetables all that much, but I try to make myself eat them. Two pounds. I could do that. I was just glad she didn't say ten. I lost ten pounds last year, just to see if I could do it. But I lost a lot of strength, so it wasn't worth it.

I sat down and laced the ribbons of my pointe shoes around my ankles. New pointe shoes look beautiful on my feet, but they feel awful. I pointed and flexed my toes, wincing.

"Is Vance here?" I stood up and gingerly rose to full pointe. I was glad it was just Miss Winnie and me. I would have died if she had talked about my weight with Vance here.

Miss Winnie glanced at a clock and frowned. "He's supposed to be, and he knows it." But the frown melted as she looked down at my feet. "New shoes, I see."

I nodded. My feet felt like they were encased in two cement blocks. To soften their shoes, some dancers do things like slam their shoes into doorways, hit them with hammers, douse them with alcohol. For me, the best way to break in new pointe shoes is simply to wear them, let them conform to the shape of my feet.

The class, if you can call it that, was excruciatingly slow. Miss Winnie had me doing *pliés* and *tendus* until my knees and toes ached. My feet felt like a sumo wrestler had put an enormous hand around each one and squeezed hard. Miss Winnie kept giving me corrections, manipulating my feet, my fingers, my standing leg. My hips were practically screaming from turning out so much. "Again," she would say. "Again." The beads of perspiration on my forehead were from frustration as much as from exertion. I wanted to dance, not just point my toes!

"This is the work you need," Miss Winnie said. "You have good training at your school, but I see you have some bad habits. You must break them if you want to improve."

So I gritted my teeth and did as she said.

We continued as Miss Winnie coached me through a full barre. My feet throbbed painfully in my new shoes. I could feel blisters forming on my middle toes. New shoes always give me blisters. When we finished, I took off my shoes and wiggled my toes, grateful to feel the air between them. I was frustrated, because it seemed like I couldn't do anything right. On the other hand, it was exciting to have someone pay such close attention to my technique.

But then I remembered what Madame Caroline had said to me when I didn't get cast as Princess Aurora, how there would always be a dancer better than me, one with more talent. I thought of sixteen-year-old girls who were already in ballet companies. I thought of the Colorado Ballet with, at most, only one or two openings per year. *Maybe this is all one big joke,* my ugly voice told me. *Maybe you can't do it.*

Miss Winnie seemed to sense my mood, because she gave me a little nod, like she wanted to know what I was thinking.

"Sometimes it all seems so impossible," I said. "I don't know. . . ."

"I can't believe for you," Miss Winnie said gently. "But I can believe with you."

How could she have known exactly the right thing to say to me? I couldn't really explain it, but it was like a tiny pinpoint of light amid all my doubts, all my insecurities. And she had said I was talented, that I was worth coaching. I felt myself smiling. Maybe I can do this. Maybe I will.

six

When Bridget and I arrived at the studio on Monday, Camilla, Ursula, and some of the younger girls were crowded around the bulletin board.

"What's going on?" I asked as Bridget and I joined them.

"Remember that guy from class Wednesday?" Camilla said. "He's gonna be the Prince in *Sleeping Beauty.*"

"Vance?" There it was, *Vance Ross, Prince,* penciled in under Anna's name as Princess Aurora. Vance, who had scoffed at the men from the Colorado Ballet, who didn't show up for Sunday's class with Miss Winnie, had agreed to be the Prince in our spring performance?

"Even more reason for you to be Princess Aurora," Bridget said. "Anna'll look like Casper the Ghost next to him."

Camilla chuckled. "Interracial fairy tale. That'll turn some heads for sure!"

I shrugged. The casting was Madame Caroline's decision, not mine.

Bridget pointed to the board. "Summer program auditions start in two weeks."

"Screw that," Camilla said with a nasty, phlegmy-sounding cough. "Those things suck! You go in, you're given a number, and you get herded around like cattle."

"If they even look at you at all," Ursula said gloomily.

"Some of them even use the process of elimination," Camilla went on. "Someone takes one look at you, and if they don't like what they see, it's 'Thank you very much.' "

I studied the list of ballet schools. Boston, San Francisco, Pacific Northwest, Houston, and, of course, the most prestigious, New York City's School of American Ballet. I spent the past few summers at a dance camp in Aspen. I met girls from all over the country and spent six weeks taking three dance classes a day. Most importantly, I had a scholarship. But this summer I really needed to go to a summer program attached to a major ballet company. At the end of summer sessions, some dancers are invited to stay for the school year, which gives them a better chance of being accepted into the company. The major programs hold auditions all over the country, picking the best of the best for their summer sessions. Before I could shut it out, my ugly voice sneered, *What makes you think you can even make the cut?* I gritted my teeth and thought about Miss Winnie's encouraging words yesterday. Staring at the audition notices on the bulletin board, that feeling of hope I had yesterday wavered like the flame of a birthday candle in a sudden gust of wind.

"Which auditions are you going to, Stephanie?" Bridget asked.

I didn't answer.

"This whole ballet thing is getting stupid," Camilla said. "I mean, you take class every day, your feet hurt, your muscles ache, and for what? Who here's good enough to really make it? Or even make it into the back line of some corps de ballet somewhere?"

"How can you say that?" Ursula said, horrified.

Camilla laughed. "Yeah, right, like you could ever be a dancer with your body."

Ursula's eyes glistened. She ran to the dressing room. We all watched, stunned.

Camilla just shrugged. "You think I'm not telling the truth? What ballet company would take her? Or me for that matter?"

"Your legs go on forever," Bridget said.

Camilla kicked one leg in front of her. "Yeah, with Donald Duck feet attached."

I left the argument and went to the dressing room. Ursula was sitting by herself in a corner. Not crying, but staring out into space. Her face, so plain compared to Camilla's, was full of misery. Anna was there, too, braiding her hair. She must have snuck by all the commotion in the lobby.

"Hey . . ." I sat down next to Ursula.

"I hate her sometimes." Ursula's voice was barely audible. Her eyes welled up and a tear trickled down her face.

"That's just Camilla." I put an arm around her, and she leaned against my shoulder.

"Sure, she can talk like that. She's got guys calling her from the moment she gets home from ballet. She can just quit and have a normal life. But what about me?" Ursula's voice broke, and she put her face in her hands. Her shoulders shook.

I didn't know what to do. I looked up at Anna, who had stopped braiding her hair.

"What would I do if I didn't take class every day?" Ursula sat up, red-faced. "But I look in the mirror sometimes and I just hate this body! I hate it! No turnout, no extension—" She swiped a fierce hand across her face.

"Ursula—"

Camilla entered the dressing room, laughing about something. She put on her ballet shoes and tied a skirt around her slender waist while Ursula sat shaking. Why was fate so unfair? Camilla didn't really give a damn about ballet, even though she came to class every day. Why did she have the better body than Ursula for ballet?

All during barre, I tried to work the way Miss Winnie had shown me yesterday, paying close attention to correct technique. The problem was, I couldn't keep up with Madame Caroline's rapid-fire combinations.

Madame Caroline stood next to me during a *frappé* exercise. "Having trouble today?"

I shook my head and kept going.

Madame Caroline told the accompanist to stop playing. The room was silent as all eyes turned to me. "Then why are you doing your own choreography?"

I took a deep breath. "I was just trying to work correctly."

Madame Caroline turned to Anna. "Anna, do a *frappé*. One single *frappé*."

Blank-faced, Anna did as she was told, striking her foot on the floor to an extended leg and pointed toe.

"There." Madame Caroline walked over to Anna. "That's what I want to see from everyone. And in the combination I gave."

I could feel the tension in my clenched neck and shoulders.

Madame Caroline called on Anna to demonstrate nearly

every combination in center floor. After class, when we all went to the dressing room to change into our pointe shoes, Camilla grumbled, "What's this, 'I love Anna' day or something?" No one answered, but we all felt grim. I laced on my pointe shoes and stood up. My shoes felt a little less like cement blocks today after working in them with Miss Winnie.

On Monday, we have variations class, in which we learn brief solos from the classical repertoire. Madame Caroline began today's class by saying, "We're going to start learning a variation from the Grand Pas de Deux of *Sleeping Beauty.* Anna will be performing it in the spring concert." Madame Caroline demonstrated the steps, then immediately began working with Anna, telling her how to move her arms and shoulders.

At the back of the room, Camilla leaned against the barre.

"Are you with us, Camilla?" Madame Caroline asked.

"I didn't know this was a rehearsal for Anna," Camilla said dryly.

"If you'd rather not join us, that's your choice." Madame Caroline turned to Ursula and Bridget and motioned for them to demonstrate. The two of them danced the opening section of the variation, stumbling where they were uncertain.

"Lengthen, Ursula," Madame Caroline said. "Your arms look like chicken wings."

When I turned to the barre again, Camilla was gone.

Camilla wasn't in class on Tuesday and, surprisingly enough, neither was Anna. Anna was absent again on Wednesday.

"Maybe the new favorite jumped ship," Camilla said on Wednesday as she laced on her pointe shoes for partnering class.

Yesterday had been a much-needed day off. "I was sick of Madame Caroline's b.s.," she told us.

But today was a good day because we had a guest teacher from the Colorado Ballet. He gave me three corrections at the barre and even had me demonstrate the *pirouette* combination. I was ecstatic, but would he have noticed me if Anna had been in class?

Vance was there. Miss Winnie, too, wearing bronze this time. She gave me an encouraging wink as she watched class. Vance acted the same way as he had last week: sullen and slouching between combinations, then executing correctly when the music started.

Instead of sitting next to Vance like I did last week, when I entered the studio for partnering class, I took a spot across the room from him and stretched one leg on the barre. But I could still see Camilla saunter in, appraise the room slowly, then cozy up next to Vance.

"So I hear you're going to be the Prince in *Sleeping Beauty,*" she said.

"I'm just doing you all a favor," he said smugly.

Camilla laughed like she was in on a joke with him. "You're doing me a favor?"

"I was talking about this dance studio." Vance turned onto his side. "I don't see how you do it. This ballet stuff every day."

Camilla flexed and pointed her toes. "It's called dedication. Dedication," she repeated in a self-important way, as if she were making fun of herself. How did she do it, turn what I would have taken as an insult into a flirtatious joke?

"All you uptight rich girls . . ." Vance looked around the room as he said this. Did his eyes stop for a moment on me? A quick flash of mortification warmed my face. But I grew angry. What does he know, anyway?

Camilla smiled in a teasing way. "So why grace us uptight girls with your presence?"

Now he grinned, even more smug-looking. "You all need me. That's why."

What a jerk! I wasn't about to listen to any more of his egomania, so I walked over to Chris, who was stretching at the center barre. His black ponytail was stringy with sweat.

"Can I work with you today?" I asked him.

He took his leg off the barre and wiped his face with a dingy-looking towel. "Sure. When are you gonna come over to the Colorado Ballet, anyway?"

It was a running joke between us. When I'm good enough, is what I usually say, but today I said, "You think they'd want me?"

"Sure." He said it so automatically that I wasn't sure if he was just being nice or if he really meant it. He backed away from me and extended an arm. "Let's try that butterfly lift."

Knowing I could trust him, I leaped into the air. Moments later, I was held aloft over his head, my arms outstretched and my ankles crossed. It was a scary feeling, being held so high in the air, with only a hand on each side of my hipbones supporting me. If I tipped forward too far, I'd fall on my head. If my legs weren't lifted high enough behind me, I'd slither to the floor, making Chris fall with me.

The guest teacher immediately came up to us and told me to pull up from the waist. My abdominal muscles strained as I pulled up as high as I could. But the effect was beautiful. In the mirror, I looked like a bird in flight. Well, almost, anyway.

Chris lowered me to the ground. "Good job," he said. I glanced over at Vance, who still lay sprawled on the floor. I knew he couldn't lift me like that, hold me so securely.

During class, Vance partnered Camilla. They goofed up a lot—Camilla would fall off pointe, Vance would lose his grip on a supported turn, and they would both capsize. At one point, Camilla's hair fell out of its topknot and fanned over Vance's face as they tumbled to the floor. They burst out laughing as Camilla gathered her hair and hastily pinned it up again. Vance helped her to her feet and his hand lingered on her waist. It was annoying, watching them. What kind of Prince would Vance make if he couldn't take class seriously?

Camilla kept smiling up at Vance, swatting him playfully when he made a mistake. I couldn't help but wonder how she did it, make Vance smile in a way that showed he genuinely liked her. And his attitude made me think that he probably didn't genuinely like many people. But it wasn't just Vance; she'd had Sidney smiling and laughing with her last week and Chris the week before. Even with Chris, whom I've worked with a lot this year, I always felt flustered and embarrassed when I made a mistake.

After class, Miss Winnie came straight to me. "This Sunday we'll work on *pirouettes.*"

"Pirouettes?" Pirouettes came easily to me.

"I'll make sure my nephew is there this time." She looked over at Vance, who had an arm around Camilla's waist. Vance waved back. "I could wring his neck sometimes," she said under her breath. I stared at the floor, uncomfortable. The way she said that, leaning toward me, it was almost like she was divulging a secret.

After saying good-bye, I went to the dressing room and took off my pointe shoes. It felt nice to stretch my bare feet on the cold floor. Pointe shoes can feel like prison sometimes.

Ursula entered the dressing room. "Has anyone seen my sister?"

"I saw her leave with that guy," Bridget said.

Ursula's mouth fell open. "She left with him? You saw them?"

"Yeah. I saw them going up the steps together."

The younger girls were looking at one another in shock. But it was more than shock, really. I imagined everyone crowding around Camilla tomorrow to find out what'd happened. We joke around sometimes and say we're all nuns in the Order of Ballet.

Ursula sat on a bench and began untying her pointe shoes. "Well, if she gets in trouble it's her own fault."

"Maybe he just drove her home," one of the younger girls said.

"Or she drove him. I'll bet she took the car." Ursula and Camilla share a Honda Civic.

When we were dressed, I went with Ursula up the stairs to the parking lot, where Ursula frowned at an empty spot. "That witch! How'm I supposed to get home?"

"My mom'll take you." Just as I said it, Mom drove up. I couldn't help but feel a little irritated as Mom parked at the curb. It would be so great to have my own car, even if I had to share it with someone else. A car gives you so much more freedom.

As I sank onto the front seat I asked, "Can we drop off Ursula? Her sister took her car."

"That's no problem," Mom said, and Ursula got into the

backseat. She gave directions to her house, a nice-looking suburban home in one of those picket-fence neighborhoods not too far from the studio. As Mom drove to Ursula's house, I couldn't help but picture Vance and Camilla together. Maybe he was one of those black guys who dated only white girls. But then again, Camilla's Camilla. She could probably wrap any guy around her finger.

After we dropped off Ursula, I told Mom I was going to Miss Winnie's house again on Sunday. Mom's lips tightened a little, which irked me.

"Mom, she thinks I'm good."

"I just don't see how she can keep teaching you without expecting payment," Mom said.

"Mom!" I exclaimed. "Didn't you hear her say she wanted to teach me? She thinks I'm good. Why can't you just believe that!"

Mom nodded a little, but it seemed more like resignation than agreement to me. We were silent the rest of the drive home. What could I say? If I discussed ballet, Mom wouldn't know what I was talking about. I wish she would watch a class of mine now and then—not be a pushy ballet mother, but just get to know something about what I do. Maybe then she would understand what ballet meant to me, how important it was to have someone believe I have talent.

At home, I found two more college catalogs on my bed, from Rice and the University of Colorado. The Colorado catalog was opened to a section on the dance department. I shut it and put them both in my bottom desk drawer. But thankfully, Dad didn't say anything about them during dinner.

seven

"Don't think. Just do!" Miss Winnie instructed.

I placed my feet into fifth position and spun, stumbling as I landed.

"You must land in a perfect fifth position," Miss Winnie said. "Again!"

I could do multiple *pirouettes,* but I didn't always land them perfectly. I could finish a *pirouette* in a deep fourth position lunge—that was easy. But landing in fifth position with my feet wedged together, heel to toe, toe to heel, was much more difficult. Sweat flew off my forehead as I turned on pointe, sometimes rotating too much, sometimes too little. Vance was turning next to me with similar problems. I watched him stumble off a *pirouette* and swear.

"Vance Ross!" Miss Winnie said in a way that made me want to giggle.

My *pirouettes* were getting worse, not better.

"You're thinking too much," Miss Winnie said.

I understood that. Once you psyched yourself out, you couldn't do anything anymore. And *pirouettes* were extremely sensitive to the psyche.

Vance, attempting five rotations, fell hard on his rump.

"That's the worst that can happen," Miss Winnie said as Vance picked himself up, scowling. "You can't be afraid to fall. I saw Suzanne Farrell fall on stage once."

I gasped. Falling on stage is one of my worst nightmares. And Suzanne Farrell was one of my favorite ballerinas.

"There she was in a beautiful white tutu, in *arabesque* with her partner. She reached too far and fell to the ground. But it was better that she fall attempting something wonderful than hold back. Let's take a break." Miss Winnie left the room.

My feet were screaming for mercy. I sat down and took off my pointe shoes. Vance sprawled on the floor beside me. His T-shirt clung to his sweaty torso. I concentrated on rubbing my feet, pointing and flexing my toes. I kept stealing glances his way, but Vance just lay there like a dead man, saying nothing. His legs, bare beneath his gym shorts, were stretched out in front of him. He had great legs for a dancer—with tapered, well-defined muscles. His ballet slippers were ratty and gray—I couldn't tell if they once had been white or black.

The silence was excruciating, so I just sat there rubbing my feet. What could I say? And yet there was so much I was curious about. If ballet was so stupid to him, then why did he try so hard in class? And why was he trying so hard today, doing *pirouette* after *pirouette*?

"So, she teaches you every Sunday?" I asked.

Vance nodded, shutting his eyes. So much for my attempt at conversation.

But then music flooded the room from an unseen source. We hadn't worked with music before. I looked around but saw no stereo. The music sounded familiar—haunting, quiet at first, lushly romantic, building to a loud crescendo that practically shook the walls. It was music I'd heard in a ballet before. It was difficult to count because it wasn't in a square meter I was used to hearing in ballet class. And then in my mind rose an image of Leslie Browne and Mikhail Baryshnikov in an otherwise empty studio, dancing a romantic pas de deux in the movie *The Turning Point. The Turning Point* is almost every ballet student's favorite movie. We all watched it at a sleep-over at Bridget's house a few months ago.

Miss Winnie appeared in the doorway as the music melted into a softly descending finish. She was smiling. She held a remote-control pad. "I'll play it again." Moments later, music again surged through the house. It was like an ocean lapping over me in gentle waves. I shut my eyes and lay on the floor, imagining myself leaping around a large expanse of space. The music made me think of a starlit night, with the moon casting a shimmery glow. I would be wearing a gauzy dress, sheer and light. My partner would reach out to me and—

"Hey!" Vance shouted, ending my lovely daydream.

"What?" I had to shout to make myself heard over the music. A doorbell rang in the distance. Miss Winnie had left the room.

Vance stood up. "Come on, this'll be funny."

I followed him to the front door.

"Will you please turn that music down?" I could hear someone saying.

"Why don't you come in and take class, Terrell?" Miss Winnie said. When she stepped aside, I could see a skinny boy in an oversize Lakers shirt. He looked about twelve.

"I don't wanna be no ballerina!" He ran away from the door.

"Does this happen a lot?" I whispered to Vance.

"Just about every Sunday," he said as Miss Winnie turned down the volume of her stereo. "Someone always comes by to tell her to turn down the music. Look here." He beckoned me to follow him to the living room window and pointed to the house across the street, where three little girls sat playing with dolls on the cramped front lawn. An older woman wearing a housecoat and slippers sat on a front porch, watching them. "Sometimes when Miss Winnie's got the music real loud, those little girls start spinning around and stuff. It's funny."

"Does she make the neighbors angry?"

"Nah. They just think she's weird, that's all." For once, Vance didn't have a smug, I-don't-give-a-damn look on his face. "What?"

I blinked. I must have been staring at him. "Nothing . . ." I was saved from saying anything else because Miss Winnie called us into the kitchen.

She had a tray of tiny sandwiches set on the table, cut in neat rectangles. The sandwiches were arranged carefully on a bed of lettuce and looked decorative more than edible. I had to wonder why anyone would go through so much trouble just for sandwiches.

"Lunchtime," Miss Winnie said. She took a pitcher from the refrigerator.

"Did you make this?" I asked.

"Like Miss Winnie ever cooks!" Vance said.

"I do cook." Miss Winnie sat at the table with us. "Sometimes."

She put five sandwiches on a plate for each of us. She also poured us glasses of iced tea from the pitcher. The tea was unsweetened, but I didn't ask for sugar.

"What was that music?" I asked before biting into a cucumber sandwich.

"*Romeo and Juliet.* It's the balcony scene from Prokofiev's score."

"I remember it from *The Turning Point.*"

"I'm going to choreograph a pas de deux for you and Vance to that music."

Vance was looking at Miss Winnie strangely. "What for?"

"It will be good for you both."

"So what do you do here, Miss Winnie?" I asked her.

"Oh, that depends—"

"Dance groupie," Vance put in.

Miss Winnie laughed. "Oh, hush! I'm retired. I try to train this knucklehead. He doesn't know how gifted he is. He prefers wasting his time at nightclubs with his friends."

I wanted to know more, but Miss Winnie said, "We'll begin the pas de deux in an hour. You need time to digest your lunch. In the meantime, we'll watch a video."

She moved us to a sitting room on the second floor. I call it a sitting room because its only pieces of furniture were two high-back armchairs, which were covered with a blue velvety material, and a television set. Miss Winnie instructed us to sit in the chairs, and she put a video into the VCR. Then, surprisingly, she left the room, leaving us alone to watch the video.

I'd seen the video before; it was a tape of the Dance Theatre of Harlem performing a mix of classical and contemporary works. But it was weird, sitting there, just Vance and me. I wondered where Miss Winnie went. I wanted to fold my legs under me, but my legs kept slipping on the velvety chair. Keeping my head faced forward, I looked askance to see what Vance was doing. He seemed to be watching the video, but his face showed no expression, none that I could see, anyway. So I focused on the video.

My favorite ballet was called *Holberg Suite,* a classical piece set to the music of Edvard Grieg, featuring girls in pale chiffon dresses and boys in regal-looking tunics and tights. I forgot all about Vance as I got caught up in the beauty of the piece. Unlike the members of traditional ballet companies, the girls in the Dance Theatre of Harlem wear tights and pointe shoes dyed to match the shade of their skin tone. It was a beautiful effect; it seemed to extend the classical lines—the shape of the movement created by the dancers. At one point, the camera panned in close to a very dark-skinned dancer's face as she lifted her eyes upward. I gasped a little, realizing I had stopped breathing for a moment. The brief image of her face on the screen, so full of love and dedication, was like a beam of light. I pressed my fingertips sharply into the arms of my chair. I wanted to jump through the television and join the company, right then and there.

I glanced over at Vance, but he didn't seem to be watching at all. He blinked slowly, sleepy-eyed, almost like he could have been staring at any random program on TV. How could he be so nonchalant? I didn't understand it.

We didn't do much pas de deux work after the video had ended. Vance still didn't know enough about partnering, so Miss Winnie just had us practice supported *pirouettes* and *promenades.* I landed on the floor a lot. It was partially my fault—

I didn't always know how to find and maintain my balance. Dancing with a partner looks so easy on stage, but the truth is, it takes so much time and effort to develop proper timing and balance. But all Miss Winnie would say was, "Try again, dear. Try again."

It was late afternoon by the time Miss Winnie decided we were finished for the day. My body ached and my ribs were sore, but I felt good. I buttoned a shirt over my leotard; Vance pulled on a pair of raggedy sweatpants.

"I can give you a ride home," he said, "take you to Beverly Hills, or wherever."

I blinked, unable to respond. I mean, how could he possibly think I was rich? Then I remembered his seeing me in my school uniform. Talk about jumping to conclusions!

"Drive carefully," Miss Winnie told him before giving me a warm smile. "I'll see you next Sunday."

"Okay," I said and thanked her for working with me. So this was how it was going to be: Sunday afternoons at Miss Winnie's house. I loved the thought of it.

Vance led me out to the carport, to a burgundy sedan. To my surprise, he opened the car door for me, then closed it behind me. I didn't know guys really did that. Miss Winnie must have told him to. But he didn't make a big deal of it. He just trudged around to the driver's side and slumped in the front seat. His forehead was shiny, and he looked tired.

The car's interior smelled like Miss Winnie's perfume, peppermints, and velvet. The radio was tuned to a classical music station. I expected Vance to change the station to something else, but instead he just shut it off. We drove in silence.

"Miss Winnie lets you drive her car," I said, mainly to fill the silence.

He nodded slightly. "Where do you live?"

"Make a left up here." I motioned him onto a main street. "Where do you live?"

"Sometimes I stay at my mom's, sometimes at Miss Winnie's."

"Where does your mom live?"

"Up the street a ways. Not far. I'll bet you live in a mansion."

"Why would you think that?"

"All this ballet stuff. It's rich-girl stuff."

"Why is it rich-girl stuff?"

"For one, it's expensive. And two, it's classical. Only rich people do classical stuff. It's white people stuff."

"Miss Winnie does it!"

"Yeah, well, Miss Winnie's foggy in the head sometimes."

What a rude thing to say! I motioned for him to go straight. "And what about Arthur Mitchell? What about the Dance Theatre of Harlem?"

"They're crazy."

I was getting mad. "Oh, so you think black people can do only certain things?"

"I never said that—"

"Yes, you did, if you said black people shouldn't do ballet!"

"Whatever."

I sat back for a moment and crossed my arms. Whatever. People say that when they don't want to listen to you talk anymore. Maybe he thought I was being bitchy. But I couldn't let the conversation go. Not yet.

I sat up again. "What would you do if you didn't dance, then?"

"Huh?"

"Would you be a basketball player? A rap star?"

Vance glanced at me like he thought I was crazy.

"Let's see, what else could you do? You could open a soul-food restaurant—"

"I get your point!"

"I mean it! What would you do if you didn't dance?"

"I don't know!" Vance cut off his words like he was definitely finished talking to me. So once again, an uncomfortable silence filled the car.

Just for the heck of it, I had him drive us through a neighborhood in Cherry Hills Village, right past my school. Vance's eyes widened and the car slowed to a practical crawl as he gaped at the houses. "This is something!"

"Tell me about it," I said under my breath. I don't think he heard me, though.

He shook his head. "No wonder."

"No wonder what?"

"You seem so . . . I don't know, high-class or something."

I laughed out loud at that one. "Me?" What planet did he live on? I motioned for him to turn again, and we left my school's neighborhood.

"Where's your house?" Vance asked.

It was my turn to be smug. "You're almost there." I looked out the windows at the small, ordinary houses filled with ordinary people. I pointed to a beige box of a house up ahead and told Vance to stop. Dad was sweeping the driveway with a broom. He stopped what he was doing when he saw Vance's car pull up.

Vance's eyes grew wide once again, and his mouth fell open. I didn't know what to think about that. Was he disappointed somehow? But even that made me feel . . . I don't know. I get so sick of feeling out of place all the time.

"Thanks for the ride." I didn't look back as I stepped out of the car and walked up the driveway. I said a hasty hello to Dad without stopping. I was practically to the door by the time I heard the hum of the car engine as Vance drove away.

eight

To my surprise, Gillian sat next to me on Monday during study hall.

I looked at her, sort of wary. I wondered what she wanted from me.

"I just wanted to ask you . . ." Gillian paused, tucking a loose strand of curly black hair behind her ear. "Kelly's having a party at her house Friday night. Wanna come?"

I blinked, wondering if I'd heard her right.

"Her parents are going out of town. She's gonna have a keg."

"Oh . . ." Except for wine at Christmas, I never drank alcohol. And I'd never been to a party like the one Kelly was having.

"It'll be cool."

"Well, I have ballet—"

"All night?"

"Until seven or so."

"The party won't start before then. C'mon, it'll be fun!"

I didn't know what to say. I had no idea why she was inviting me in the first place.

Gillian leaned closer and lowered her voice. "More of us should be there, you know?"

"Us?"

She picked up my pen and scribbled two black dots on the sheet of blank paper I had in front of me. "That's what it feels like around here, sometimes."

I got her point. "What was your old school like?"

Gillian shrugged. "Like this. Whiteyville. I just get so sick of it sometimes. I wish I went to public school."

I did, too, but for different reasons. It was easier to just be anonymous at a public school, especially if some of the kids were rich and some weren't. Also, I imagined the schoolwork would be easier. "Why don't you go to public school?"

"Because this school's the best." She sounded bitter.

It was weird, hearing her talk like that. It wasn't as if Gillian was an outcast. She was friends with two of the most popular girls at school.

"What do you do for a social life, anyway?" Gillian asked.

I shrugged off the question, hoping I didn't look as embarrassed as I felt. "I'm so busy with ballet, I don't have much time."

Gillian looked impressed. "You're really serious about it?" When I nodded, she said, "I can tell. You look like a dancer. But why ballet, though?"

"What?"

"Why not modern, or African dance?"

"I like ballet." I'd taken some modern-dance classes in Aspen last summer. I liked them, but I liked ballet more. As for African dance, I've never done it.

Gillian drummed her fingers on the desk. "Well, I just wanted to know if you'd go to the party with me."

"I don't have a car—"

"I'll pick you up."

"And I don't know when I have to be home—" I didn't even know if I'd have a curfew or not.

"Why don't you spend the night at my house?" Gillian interrupted me. "I don't have a curfew. I'll pick you up from your ballet or whatever."

She said it like the decision had been made. Before I could say anything else, Lisa called, "Hey, Gillian!" and she quickly left to join forces with Kelly and Lisa.

I told Bridget about the party during lunch. She listened with wide eyes.

"It sounds cool," Bridget said. "Maybe Bret Carlson'll be there." She glanced across the room at a handsome, dark-haired senior sitting at a table with Kelly and Lisa. Bridget turned away quickly, almost as if she was afraid to look too long. "He's gorgeous!" she whispered, although there was no way he could have heard her across the noisy lunchroom.

I shrugged. If you liked the beefy type, I supposed. Bret played lacrosse: Lakeview doesn't have a football team, so lacrosse has the status football would have at a public school. The games are major social events in the fall. I've never gone. I always have ballet class, and besides, who would I go to a lacrosse game with, anyway?

I watched Gillian cross the room to join Lisa, Kelly, and Bret, bringing a few guys with her. She tossed her hair in the way I've seen white girls do when they flirt with guys, a flip of the hair with a coy smile. In her uniform, standing among the best-looking kids at the school, and probably the ones with the most money, too, Gillian didn't look like a black dot on a white page to me. She was pretty in the same Noxzema-commercial kind of way as Kelly and Lisa. She looked like she *belonged.*

"You'll have to tell me all about the party," Bridget said.

"Why don't you come?"

Bridget's eyes widened. "Oh, no!" Her face reddened. "I mean—no!" Outside of ballet, she's really shy.

Bridget's blush disappeared. "I can't believe Anna missed three days of class last week! What's her deal, anyway?"

"I have no idea."

"It's gonna be . . ." Bridget paused, as if she was searching for the right words ". . . weird, having that new guy dance with her. You should be Princess Aurora. You'd look great with him!"

I didn't answer. I thought of the pas de deux Miss Winnie had planned for Vance and me. So far, I hadn't said anything to anyone at the studio about her coaching me. It was my little secret.

"Of course we have rehearsal Friday night," Camilla was saying as I entered the dressing room before ballet class. Anna was sitting in a corner, sewing ribbons onto a new pair of pointe shoes.

"It's probably because that's when all the guys can come," said one of the younger girls.

"I hear they're going to get a weight lifter to be the last Cavalier," Camilla said.

"Why not get another guy from the Colorado Ballet?" Bridget asked.

"Can't pay 'em enough, probably," Camilla said. "Oh well, maybe I can make some Friday-night plans with one of the guys."

"The new guy? The guy who's gonna be the Prince?" Bridget asked.

"Not my type," Camilla said.

I kept my face blank, remembering how she flirted with Vance during partnering class. "Why do you say that?"

"He's a little too stuck on himself for my taste."

"You've already found out, huh?" Ursula muttered.

Camilla ignored her. "You should go for him, Steph."

"Why, if he's stuck on himself?" I asked.

"Maybe he'll be different with you."

Bridget gasped. "Camilla!"

"What? We just went out once, that's all. No big deal!"

"But once is all it takes with you, right!" Ursula spat out.

Camilla twisted her hair into a bun. "At least I know how to get a guy."

The tension in the room was undeniable. Bridget stared at a wall. Anna continued sewing her ribbons, but the tips of her ears were pink. We all fell silent as we got ready for class. Ursula's mouth was twisted, like she was in pain. Camilla hummed to herself. But I was curious, too, about what had happened between Camilla and Vance. Even though I'd never say it out loud, a little part of me was glad that nothing was going on between them.

nine

Our first rehearsal Friday night was chaotic; we didn't get much done. We began with the entrance of the five Fairies during the Prologue, when the baby Princess is given her gifts before the Evil Fairy says she'll prick her finger on a spindle and die. Sure enough, Madame Caroline had recruited Marty, a weight lifter who'd never danced before, to be the last Cavalier. He was good-looking, with tousled blond hair and rippling muscles. He looked like he was in his early twenties to me. The story was, he was a neighbor of Chris Martinez's and agreed to help us out. I saw a grin form at the corners of Camilla's mouth when he came into the studio in shorts and bare feet, red-faced and bewildered-looking.

"I'll work with Marty," Camilla said. "I can show him what to do."

I was paired with Chris. Vance partnered a tiny girl named

Elizabeth. The Cavaliers appear only in the Prologue, so all of the guys were doing double-duty. Only the three of us paired with the guys from Colorado Ballet could manage the big overhead lift by which all the Fairies enter. Madame Caroline had Chris and me demonstrate it over and over again. The weight lifter kept trying to bench-press Camilla.

She giggled and said, "No, not like that."

I was nervous all through rehearsal. The party was tonight, and Gillian was picking me up at the studio. I had thought my parents would give me the third degree over the party, but they were excited.

"Have a good time," Mom said.

"Be careful," Dad said. "You know what kind of behavior we expect from you."

I was miffed. It's not like I ever did anything that would really get me in trouble. How could I, with all of my ballet classes and rehearsals?

"That hurts!" Elizabeth squealed as Vance tried to lift her. He set her down and crossed his arms in frustration. Elizabeth rubbed her rib cage.

"Stephanie, come try this lift with Vance." Madame Caroline was starting to look frustrated, too.

Vance looked like he was about to storm out of the room. "Forget it. I can't do it."

"Look," I said. "I jump, and you use my upward momentum to lift me."

"Aren't you afraid I'll drop you?"

"No." I was afraid, actually, but I decided to go for it anyway. So I jumped, felt his hands on my waist, and then I was up in the air, over his head. His arms straightened. My left leg was behind me in arabesque. Vance wobbled a bit, but then stood firm.

The rest of the dancers applauded as Vance walked around the room with me posed over his head, but when I looked in the mirror, I saw terror frozen on my face. He wasn't holding me as securely as he should have been. It was perilous, traveling so close to the ceiling like that.

Coming down was rough. He brought me down too fast, and we both tumbled to the floor. But neither of us was hurt. He gave me a little half-smile, maybe as a way of saying he was sorry. I gave him a little half-smile back, and he helped me to my feet.

Rehearsal ended without our accomplishing much as a group.

"So what's going on tonight?" Camilla asked as we changed clothes.

"I'm going to a party." I tried to keep my voice light.

"Oh yeah? Where?"

"At the house of this girl from my school."

"Cool. Is it invite only?"

"I don't know. We can ask the girl who invited me."

Camilla followed me to the lobby once we were both dressed. Gillian was waiting for me. She looked glamorous to me; she wore black jeans and a tight black tank top with high black boots. Her lips were bright red and shiny. Standing there in my sweater and jean skirt, I suddenly felt like her kid sister.

Gillian had been looking into the studio through the window, but she turned around when she saw us. In the studio, Vance and Elizabeth were still practicing the lift. Gillian looked excited when she saw me. "Who's that guy in there?"

"Vance. He's gonna be the Prince in *Sleeping Beauty.*"

"I saw him lift you up. Awesome! So what's his deal?"

"I don't know."

"He have a girlfriend?"

"He's taken," Camilla cut in, then winked at me. She unpinned her hair and blond waves fell down her back. She gave Gillian the same slow appraisal that Gillian was giving her, a look of casual boredom on her face. "So where's the party?"

"You wanna come?" Gillian asked. Apparently, Camilla added up. She gave Camilla directions, and I stood there wondering how they seemed to connect so soon. Camilla must have communicated cool somehow. Was it her attractiveness? Her smoky voice? Her casual-bored look that mirrored Gillian's? I imagined Ursula asking about the party. Would Gillian's answer have been different?

"Your friend's cool," Gillian said as we walked out to her car. I felt myself tense up as I sat in the front seat of her gold Mercedes. I'll bet this car cost more than my parents' house. The inside was messy, with soiled napkins, battered school folders, and empty Diet Coke cans scattered on the floor.

"I've known Camilla a long time."

"I'll bet all you dancers hang out together." Gillian started the car. Barbie-doll music, Camilla would call it, blared from the speakers.

"Sometimes . . ." My edgy feeling intensified as Gillian drove into Kelly's neighborhood. I don't know, maybe it was the casualness of it all—the way she treated her Mercedes like it was my parents' old Ford Tempo—that bothered me. I resisted the urge to squirm in my seat. After all, it wasn't like Gillian and I had ever hung out together, or even had more than a superficial conversation. In truth, I really didn't know what to say to her.

"What was your old school like?" My voice wavered a little. I cleared my throat.

Gillian shrugged. "Boring. Just like Lakeview."

"Boring?" I said, mainly so she would keep talking.

"Same old kids spending Mommy and Daddy's money, same old gossip, same old parties . . ." Gillian glanced at me. "How long have you been going to Lakeview?"

"Since third grade."

"Yeah, so you know the score."

I didn't say anything to that. When you're younger, you don't notice things like who has money and who doesn't. Maybe you do, but it's different once you start junior high and everyone starts getting into boys. But it's not just money. Once everyone started getting into boys, that's when things really started to change for me at school. That's when I started feeling more like an outsider. First of all, I started getting serious about ballet, so I didn't have time to hang out after school. But then, how could I really get into boys when there were only two black boys in the Upper School?

"You have a lot of friends at Lakeview," I said.

Gillian shrugged, like it didn't matter. "I guess so." She parked in front of a palatial house, set off from the street on a sloping hill. It was a pale rose color, with arched windows in front. Jeeps, sport utilities, and convertibles lined the street. I gulped, my heart pounding.

"You always wear your hair like that?" Gillian asked.

My hair was still up in a bun from rehearsal. If I tried to take my hair down, it would stick out wildly in all directions, like a messy Afro. "Why do you ask?"

"It's the only style I've ever seen on you."

"I have ballet every day. It's easier to do my hair in the mornings."

"You should let me try to do something with it. I could do your makeup, too."

"I usually don't wear any—"

"You should. I mean, you could look so much older."

"Why would I want to look older?"

Gillian looked a little exasperated. "So you can go out with older guys! There'll be some college guys at the party. Do you have a boyfriend?"

"Not right now." I didn't add that I'd never had a boyfriend, never been on a date. I've never even been kissed. Whenever I think about that, I feel like a freak.

I hadn't been to Kelly's house in a few years, but what I remembered of it was pretty amazing. Kelly and her sister had their own wing. The door was unlocked, and we went in. There were kids in every room, clustered in small groups. Rap music thumped and boomed from a stereo. Almost everyone had a plastic cup in hand.

Gillian put on a bored, too-cool-for-this-place look as she walked in. She immediately took a cigarette from a pack of Marlboros in her purse and stuck it in her mouth. "Want one?" She held out the pack to me.

I shook my head quickly. My heart pounded painfully in my chest. I wanted to turn around and leave. We walked through a high-ceilinged entryway into a kitchen. Gillian paused to exchange hellos with several people. No one really paid any attention to me.

Kelly and Lisa were holding court in the kitchen, sitting on a countertop surrounded by guys. I recognized only two of them from school. One was Bret Carlson, the guy Bridget had drooled over. I don't think I've ever said one word to him.

"Gillian!" Lisa called. Her hair was sleeked straight, and her eyes were red-rimmed and glassy-looking.

"Hey girl!" Gillian hoisted herself onto the counter. "Steph, can you get me a beer?"

"Um . . ." I didn't know what to do.

Kelly jerked her head toward the kitchen door. "The keg's out back."

Almost like a zombie, I went out the back door. Five guys stood around what looked like a large tin drum.

"Wanna beer?" A guy in a University of Colorado sweatshirt asked me.

"Two."

He handed me two frothy plastic cups. I don't know why I said two—I can't stand the taste of beer. I'd sipped some from my father's can last New Year's and thought it was disgusting. Oh well, I could just hold it.

Going back inside, I had to push my way through a crowd of kids. The noise was deafening. I handed a cup to Gillian. She had lit another cigarette.

"Thanks," she said, but she was in the middle of a conversation with Lisa. It was as if she'd forgotten I was there. I just stood around, feeling like a moron.

"What are you doing here?"

I realized Bret Carlson was talking to me. "What?"

"You always look so prim and proper." He squeezed the bun on top of my head.

"Bunhead!" Kelly squealed. She sounded drunk.

I felt my lips tightening.

"Only joking. She's gonna be a ballerina." I couldn't tell if Kelly was making fun of me or not.

"Gonna drink that?" Bret motioned to my beer.

I looked down at the beer, at the condensation wetting my fingers. The cup felt cold and slimy in my hands, but I didn't set it down. I looked at Gillian on the counter, but she was nodding at something Lisa was saying. Oh, why wouldn't she just say something to me, so I wouldn't have to talk to Bret!

I was saved from having to answer by a guy who turned around, saw me in his way, I guess, and said, "Who *are* you?" I'd never seen him before. He wore a T-shirt with Greek letters on it and a backward baseball cap. *Pi* was the only letter I recognized from his shirt. I figured he must've been one of the college guys Gillian was talking about, but the truth was, he didn't look any older than Bret.

To my shock, Bret flung an arm around my shoulder. I tightened my grip on the cup as some beer sloshed onto my hand. "This is one of our Lakeview scholarship students." He lowered his voice so that he sounded like the headmaster. I flinched, squirming away from him. His arm was like a heavy branch on the back of my neck. I could hardly breathe.

But Bret's arm remained planted on my shoulder. "We're corrupting her. See, if she got caught with this beer in her hand, she could get kicked out."

I looked at Bret, so appalled I couldn't even speak.

The other guy leaned close enough to me so that I could smell his sour breath. "I guess you better be careful, huh?"

I turned my face out of his breath's line of fire. My head spun, and I thought I'd choke.

But then Bret took his arm off my shoulder. "I guess your dad could get you off the hook." He looked at the other guy and nodded in my direction. "Her dad's the school janitor."

I wanted to drop dead right there. I looked up at Gillian, but she and Lisa weren't paying attention.

"Hey, if you got kicked out, you could always follow in his footsteps," the other guy said, he and Bret laughing together.

Anger boiled in my chest. My pulse raced and my chest heaved and I was squeezing the cup of beer in my hands. Before I knew it, my arm contracted, and beer splashed into Bret's face.

He stopped laughing as beer dribbled down his cheeks.

I stood frozen, mortified.

"Stephanie!" Kelly jumped down from the counter to get some paper towels.

"Geez! Can't you take a joke?" Bret exclaimed.

Tears sprang to my eyes. I turned and hurried out of the kitchen as my vision blurred over. I gritted my teeth and pushed blindly through the crowd. I wasn't sure where I was going. Coming to this party was a huge mistake; I had no way to leave without Gillian. I reached the front door and leaned against the doorframe. Luckily, no one was paying attention to me.

Right then, the door opened and Camilla walked in with two guys trailing behind her. Both of the guys had long brown hair and wore ripped jeans with grungy-looking T-shirts. Camilla was dressed like them, her hair long and straight like a hippie's. But she still managed to look carelessly beautiful.

"Stephanie, what's going on?" Camilla said.

I almost sobbed with relief from seeing a familiar face. "Hey—"

"Steph, meet Trevor and CJ." She turned to the guys she came with, who both sort of waved at me.

"Is there any food here?" Camilla asked. "This is a rich-kid party, isn't it?"

"Do they have bowls of shrimp laying around?" one of the guys asked, but he sounded mocking.

"I don't know."

"Oh well, free beer," Camilla said. She took my arm as we weaved our way through the crowd. I felt a little better with her there.

"Hey guys, go get us some beer," Camilla said without looking at them.

"None for me," I said firmly.

"You sure?" Camilla asked. I felt my face heating up, but Camilla just said, "Okay."

"It's just not my thing," I said, as if I needed an explanation.

Camilla shrugged. Gillian and Lisa were still sitting on the kitchen counter.

"Where's Ursula?" I asked.

"At home with Mommy and Daddy, probably watching Disney videos or something. Ursula's hopeless."

I was sorry I'd asked.

Camilla lit up a cigarette and surveyed the kitchen. "So these are private-school kids."

"Mostly. I don't recognize all of them."

"This is some house."

Camilla's friends returned with beer. "There's a guy with some weed out back."

"Yeah?" Camilla said.

My heart sank. So I'd be abandoned again. I certainly wasn't going to smoke pot!

Gillian and Lisa were coming our way. "Oh, there you are,"

Gillian said to me, but she immediately turned to Camilla. "Lisa, this is Camilla."

After they did all the introductions, Lisa said, "So you're a bunhead, too?"

"Hardly," Camilla said. "This body of mine's about to go on strike!"

"It just seems crazy to me," Lisa said. "Why spend all your time taking ballet?"

I felt myself getting defensive, but Camilla laughed. "Maybe I'm just crazy."

The conversation turned to the guy with weed out on the back porch. I didn't know what to do. I didn't want to stay at this party another minute. But what could I do?

I walked away from the group without anyone noticing. I could hardly hear myself think, and yet I felt all alone. It's so much lonelier to be alone in a crowd than to be by yourself. I sat on the bottom step of a spiral staircase. I thought about calling my parents, but I knew they'd ask me a lot of questions that I didn't want to answer.

Miss Winnie! I jumped to my feet as I thought of her. But I didn't have her phone number. I ran up the stairs. In the first bedroom I came to, there was a phone on the nightstand.

I dialed Information quickly, hoping Miss Winnie was listed. "May I have the number for Wilhemina Price, of Dahlia Street?"

"One moment," said the operator. I sat on the bed, relief coursing through me as the operator gave me the number.

It was after nine o'clock, but I called anyway. I hoped I wasn't waking her up.

Miss Winnie answered the phone.

"Miss Winnie?" At the sound of her voice, I started to cry.

"Stephanie? What's wrong?"

"I'm at a party and I want to leave. I don't know where to go." I was sobbing now. I couldn't help it.

Miss Winnie was silent for a moment. "Vance has my car, child. I probably won't see him until tomorrow."

I didn't speak. I sat on the bed, holding the phone and crying.

"How about this." Miss Winnie's voice was soothing. "I'll send a cab over to get you. Can you tell me where you are?"

I gave her the address.

"Don't cry. Everything will be all right."

"Thank you." My hands shook as I hung up the phone. I went to a bathroom to splash cold water on my face. I felt stupid for crying like that. With my head lowered, I went downstairs and left the house quickly. I sat on the front porch and waited for the cab, the night wind cool on my face.

ten

I left without saying good-bye to Gillian or Camilla. In the taxi, I realized I had no money. My purse, along with my dance bag, was in Gillian's car. That meant I wouldn't have pointe shoes for Sunday. But I didn't care.

When the taxi pulled up in front of Miss Winnie's house, I wanted to start crying again, but I didn't. Miss Winnie was standing on the porch in a royal blue dressing gown. Her head was wrapped in an elaborate blue scarf that glinted with gold. To me, she looked marvelous. She paid the taxi driver, then placed a hand on my arm and led me into the house. I inhaled its familiar spicy-sweet scent.

She led me into the living room, and we sat down together on one of the couches.

"I'm so glad to see you!"

She looked at the grandfather clock. "Do you need to call your parents?"

"No. I have permission to spend the night at a friend's house."

"Don't you think you should call and tell them about your change of plans?"

I sighed. "I don't want to talk to them. Not now. I just feel so . . ." The tears were coming again. "I hate it! I hate my school! I go to school with all these rich kids who live in mansions and have cars, and me, I'm just—"

I took a deep breath. "I don't know, I'm not one of them. I'm sick of feeling like a freak all the time! At least, when I'm at ballet— I know ballet isn't always fair, but dancing . . . dancing is like, I don't know . . . it's like being a part of something that's so beautiful! I love it so much, more than anything, and my parents don't understand that." My words were tumbling out. I wasn't sure if they made any sense.

But Miss Winnie just nodded, like she understood.

"I just . . . I don't know." Then I looked up at the wall, at the photographs of Miss Winnie as a young dancer. She was tall and willowy, but not impossibly skinny. Her eyes held the wise expression I saw in them now. In one picture, her arms were stretched upward. A long white dress swished around her legs, as if she had been captured in movement. It was a simple picture, beautiful, and yet at the same time sad.

"Did you ever find it?" I asked.

"What do you mean?" Miss Winnie's voice was soft like mine.

"What you were reaching for in that picture."

"In my own career . . ." Miss Winnie looked where I looked. "No."

"But you said you danced in Europe! You danced in New York!"

"I took classes at the School of American Ballet whenever I could—whenever it was possible." She smiled. "I had feet like yours, dear. Beautiful feet. I would practice in the lobby, outside the studio. The receptionist would always ask me to leave when she saw me there. But one day, Mr. Balanchine saw me and invited me in to take class. Ah, what dancers were in class that day? None you would know. Mr. Balanchine said to me later, when he started his first company in America, I don't have a place in my company for you, but why don't you try Europe?"

"Were you good enough?"

Miss Winnie looked pensive. "I wanted to be. I was never given the chance. I worked in a hotel uptown back then. Cleaning rooms and such. And I saved enough money for a one-way ticket on a boat to Europe. But the war was on.

"For six years I continued to work, to save money for Europe. And life happened to me, I suppose. I met a young man, but we didn't get married. But by the time I got to Europe, it was 1950 and my best years for dancing were already behind me."

"But you danced in Europe, right?"

"Oh yes, I danced in Europe. I was in a small company in Stuttgart for several years. That's where those pictures were taken. Germany was a shabby place after the war. You should have seen our theater!" She laughed. "The stage was so tiny. But the people came. Crowded together on folding chairs that squeaked whenever anyone moved. But when I heard the applause, I knew I'd done the right thing in coming to Europe. We even toured the Continent. Twice."

"Did you do any classical works? *Swan Lake*? *Sleeping Beauty*? *Giselle*?"

"Heavens, no." Miss Winnie chuckled. "We were a classical company, but we didn't have the people, the money, or even the skill to mount anything that ambitious. I still remember Frau Borg, our artistic director. She spoke some English because she had studied at Sadler's Wells in London before the war. She would say to me, 'You have so much heart, dear. So much heart.' She meant love."

I sank into the sofa. I guess I'd always had an image in my head of Miss Winnie on all the grand stages in Europe, bowing at her applause. All of my doubts, the doubts that had started to fade when Miss Winnie said I was talented, came flooding back. Is a professional ballet career really just an impossible dream? Could I do it, even with Miss Winnie's help, when Miss Winnie couldn't even do it herself? Miss Winnie's face, its deep lines, showed so much disappointment. So much regret.

"I came back to New York in 1956, the year Arthur Mitchell joined the New York City Ballet. I was in my thirties then, but I still managed to get a place in the New York Negro Ballet. We had one good season, but then our funding ran out."

"Why?"

"People weren't ready to see black ballet dancers in those days. Some said our bodies weren't right for ballet. For others it went against tradition. But our efforts in those days weren't a waste of time. We were laying the groundwork. George Balanchine has said that you cannot change what is inherent in an art form," Miss Winnie said. "And he said that ballerinas should have skin the color of a freshly peeled apple."

Skin the color of a freshly peeled apple? It wasn't some challenge to be met, like babying my hair with special conditioners and gentle combs to coax it into a bun every morning. It was just an obstacle. A door slammed shut and bolted tight, preventing my entrance.

I sighed. "So should I do modern dance, then?"

"If your heart is in ballet, then that's what you must do," Miss Winnie said. "But if you think it will be easy, it won't be."

"Auditions for summer programs start next week."

"For what ballet schools?"

"School of American Ballet, San Francisco, all the important ones. And I really have to audition this year. My parents told me that if I'm not accepted into a company by the time I graduate, then I have to go to college."

"You don't want to go to college?"

"I'll go later, I will. But now I want to dance! If I wait, it'll be too late, and then I'll never dance in a company!"

Miss Winnie sat silent for a moment. She turned to stare at the photographs of herself on the walls. I couldn't tell what she was thinking at all. But when she turned back to me, she was smiling.

"Times have changed. There will be many more opportunities for you than there were for me." Her smile broadened. "So that is what I must do. To prepare you and Vance for success."

I hugged her then—felt the warmth of her arms around me. That awful party seemed far away now, like a bad dream.

"Are you up to a little work?" she asked me.

"Sure, but I don't have my dance bag."

Miss Winnie got up from the couch. "I may have something for you to wear." She went upstairs, and I waited on the couch for her to return.

She came downstairs holding what looked like a gauzy dress. "It may be a little too big on you."

I looked at the picture on the wall, then down at the mound of chiffon she had placed in my arms. "You wore this?"

"I danced a short solo in this dress in nineteen fifty-two."

I examined the dress closely. It was beige, its hems yellowed with age. The sheer material felt fragile in my hands.

"I don't have any shoes, either."

"Then we'll work without them."

"Where can I change?"

"Use the bathroom down the hall. I'll put some sheets on the bed in the guest room. Meet me in the studio when you've changed."

The costume sagged around my shoulders and around my legs—Miss Winnie was much taller than me. It had been knee-length in the picture, but it was ankle-length on me. I treaded slowly as I entered the studio, enjoying the sensation of my bare feet against the smooth wood floor. How nice it felt to spread my toes as I walked, without the constriction of pointe shoes. The moon shone in through the windows, bathing the studio in a bluish-gold glow. The light caught my costume, making it shimmer.

I lifted one leg to the barre and stretched, holding the strap where it slipped off my shoulders. My legs and feet were bare, my hair still up in a bun. It was a little eerie, being in a darkened studio alone, but at the same time, it was wonderful. I began humming to myself as I did *pliés* and *tendus* to warm up. And then I began waltzing around the studio, whirling until the skirt billowed around me. From turns I began to leap to my own inner music, conscious of nothing but my own movement. A sweat broke on my skin as I whirled and leaped, higher and faster.

And then an invasive feeling came over me, like I was being watched. I stopped in the center of the room, breathing heavily.

A shadowy figure stood in the doorway. My breath caught in my throat, and I coughed. The light panels illuminated overhead, and I saw Vance in the doorway watching me.

He wore black baggy pants and a white button-down shirt. It was the first time I had seen him in anything other than sweats. Another flush came over me, over the heat of dancing. I lifted the fallen shoulder straps of Miss Winnie's costume into place. I didn't speak. I couldn't. I had no idea how long he'd been standing there.

"What are you doing here?" he asked finally.

"What are *you* doing here?" I echoed, not knowing what else to say.

"I stay here sometimes." Vance entered the studio, the hard soles of his shoes clicking on the floor. I could smell cigarette smoke on him.

"Do you smoke?"

"Me? Nah." He stopped a few feet from me and stood there.

"You smell like smoke."

"I was at a club. The Odyssey. Ever been there?"

I shook my head.

"It's just a stupid teen club. Folks get rough there sometimes. Gangs and stuff."

"Why do you go, then?"

"They had a dance contest. Me and the fellas, we put together some steps."

"Did you win?"

"Second place. Stupid contest was fixed. They gave places

based on applause. You know, whoever gets the loudest cheers from the crowd." Vance was looking at my shoulder straps, which had fallen again. "What's up with that?"

"Miss Winnie let me wear it. I didn't have anything to wear."

"So how'd you end up here tonight, anyway?"

I shook my head. "I don't want to talk about it."

"I saw you." Vance motioned behind me. "Jumping around like a demon."

So he had seen me. I turned around and went to the barre. He was making me nervous. I wanted him to leave.

But he didn't leave. I could feel him watching me as I began to do *pliés.* I felt self-conscious, yes, but what else could I do? It was easier just to dance.

I was thankful when I heard Miss Winnie enter the room. "Vance," she said. "You're home early. Oh well, let's get started."

"What?" Vance said.

I turned around so I was facing them, but I continued to do *pliés.*

"Are you warmed up?" Miss Winnie asked him.

"You must be crazy," he said.

Miss Winnie ignored that comment and came to me. "What about you, dear. Are you warmed up?"

I nodded. The muscles in my legs tingled.

Miss Winnie wanted to see my *arabesque.* I extended a leg behind me, pulling up from my abdominal muscles as straight as I could. But Miss Winnie pushed my body forward over my standing leg, then lifted my leg behind me a few inches higher.

"That's where your *arabesque* should be." She had me plunge forward into a *penchée.* My leg wasn't in a full split, nowhere near it, but she pushed my leg, showing me how much higher I could lift it with more strength.

Vance didn't leave the room. He merely watched as Miss Winnie manipulated my *arabesque,* molding my fingers, my head, my feet, my placement.

She had me come out to center floor.

"Vance, take her hand," Miss Winnie said. Vance took my hand as I stepped into *arabesque* toward him, rising on half-toe.

"Promenade her slowly—"

Vance immediately lifted his other arm so it seemed to float on the air. Slowly, he walked in a circle around me as I pivoted on my foot, using his hand for balance. His hand was warm and sweaty.

"Stretch your leg, Stephanie," Miss Winnie said.

But I was looking into Vance's eyes, and he was looking into mine. It was practical. . . . I needed something to focus on as he turned me. My standing foot grew warm from the friction of turning without shoes, but it was a warmth that radiated up my leg, into my body, and through my fingertips.

Vance held his head high, his back straight. His expression was strange—soft. He had curly eyelashes, the kind girls have only if they use eyelash tongs. He had an aristocratic face, prominent cheekbones, smooth skin. I could see the black pupils of his eyes, and the thin rim of brown around them.

Miss Winnie had us try all sorts of things. Lifts, supported turns. I could see her starting to piece things together in her head. I wore her too-large costume, Vance wore his going-out clothes, but it seemed right to me, the three of us being there, working past midnight.

At one o'clock Miss Winnie decided she was finished. She showed me upstairs to a room with a canopied bed covered with a frothy white comforter. A sheer sleeveless gown lay on the bed with a matching robe. It was gorgeous: creamy silk, edged with lace. It seemed like something a bride would wear on her wedding night. I put it on, the delicate fabric caressing my skin. It was too large for me, like the costume that now was laid out carefully on a chair. I pulled back the coverlet and got into bed. And then I thought of Vance, somewhere in this house. He must have his own room here. When Miss Winnie led me up the stairs, Vance had gone someplace else, disappeared. But the idea of him somewhere in this house . . . I didn't finish the thought. Instead, I imagined us dancing together, his walking around me in a slow promenade, looking into my eyes.

eleven

It took me a moment to remember where I was. I blinked a few times, disoriented, until the room, with its pale blue wallpaper, came into focus. A length of chiffon lay on an armchair. Miss Winnie's old costume. In the light it looked yellow more than beige, and there were mottled spots on the bodice I hadn't noticed the night before. I pulled the comforter around me. What time was it? I wasn't wearing a watch, and I didn't see a clock in the room. The sky out the window was an indeterminable gray. It could have been seven in the morning or noon. Part of me wanted to lie down against the soft pillows—they felt like goose down—and wallow in luxuriant sleep. But what if it was late? I searched for my clothing, thinking I should get dressed and go downstairs. But I didn't see my clothes anywhere.

I shut my eyes, remembering. My jean skirt and sweater

were in the downstairs bathroom. That meant I'd have to go downstairs in this nightgown. The thought made me want to bury myself under the comforter. I looked down at the shimmery fabric. It was a beautiful ivory color that looked great against my skin. But it was so sheer! I could see the outline of my legs through the material. Last night, I had thought it looked like something a bride would wear on her wedding night. But I was no bride. The thought of going downstairs like this, with Vance in the house . . .

I glimpsed a robe of matching fabric hanging over another armchair, but I didn't want to move. What would Vance say if he saw me like this? Maddeningly, there was no mirror in the room. I raised my hand to my head, feeling my hair sticking out in all directions. Oh, why didn't I have a comb when I needed one? I gathered as much hair in my hands as I could and looked around for my scrunchie, which I use to tie my hair up in its bun. I got down on my hands and knees, searching the floor. Where had I put it? Without that scrunchie, I was definitely not leaving this room!

I could hear footsteps downstairs, but no voices. Someone was up. Maybe Miss Winnie and Vance were both up and dressed, waiting for me. Panic warmed my face.

My scrunchie had rolled under the bed, and my heart raced when I grabbed it. I'd never been so happy to find a scrap of elasticized fabric in my life. I tied up my hair the best I could, then clutched the fragile robe around my shoulders. Breathing deeply, I opened the bedroom door a crack.

The hallway was clear. I stepped out of the bedroom, listening carefully. Clacking footsteps. Miss Winnie must have been wearing high heels. The whistle of a teakettle. I made my way down the stairs, as softly as I could in my bare feet. At the foot of the stairs I stopped again. The grandfather clock in the living room showed eight-twenty. Maybe Vance was still asleep. He seemed like the late-rising type to me. That thought let me breathe a little easier as I walked toward the kitchen.

Vance and Miss Winnie were both at the table as I approached. My heart sank. Vance was dressed in his usual dance-class outfit of gray sweats and white tank top. He sat splay-legged at the table, absentmindedly stirring a cup of tea. Miss Winnie was dressed as well, in a black dress with a matching wide-brimmed black hat. Her eyes followed a newspaper column. I wanted to turn around and charge upstairs to the room.

"Stephanie." Miss Winnie must have heard me. Vance looked up—I could feel him looking at me even though I kept my eyes on Miss Winnie. "Join us for breakfast."

"I will . . . after I change." I dashed out of the room before she could say anything else. I went to the bathroom, retrieved my clothes, then ran upstairs to change.

My hands shook as I removed the robe and nightgown. Maybe I had left the kitchen too quickly, looked foolish. But I felt better when I had my sweater and jean skirt on. I tried several doors until I found a bathroom, where I did a better job of smoothing down my hair.

Feeling much more composed, I headed for the kitchen, but Vance's voice made me stop halfway down the stairs.

". . . dress," he was saying. "That's messed up, Miss Winnie."

And then Miss Winnie's voice, abrupt in a way I'd never heard before. "I don't know what you're talking about."

Silence from Vance. I craned my neck toward the kitchen, straining to hear.

"Make sure you clean up those scuff marks on the studio floor," Miss Winnie went on in that same chastising voice. "You know you're not supposed to wear street shoes in the studio."

"Yeah, well I didn't expect to have dance class at midnight," Vance said snidely.

"Tracking all that filth from those . . . nightclubs . . ."

"Don't start up with that again." Vance raised his voice ever so slightly, but his anger was unmistakable.

"All the time you waste—"

"I'm going to get up and walk out that door in about thirty seconds."

The rustle of a newspaper was Miss Winnie's response. The kitchen was silent. I swallowed and approached the kitchen, walking as softly as I could. Miss Winnie had set a bowl of fruit on the table. She stared at the newspaper on the table, but after what I'd overheard, I'd bet that she was staring at the newspaper to avoid Vance. Vance hadn't moved from his slumped position. He glanced at me briefly, then stared into space.

Miss Winnie looked up. "Did you sleep well?"

"Thank you for letting me stay over last night." Once I'd said it, I wished I hadn't. It sounded feeble to me, like something to say to fill up space.

Miss Winnie set a plate in front of me, but I didn't really feel like eating. My stomach ached, probably because I hadn't eaten since lunch yesterday, but I felt too out of sorts to eat right now.

I didn't know what to say. The easy camaraderie we'd all had last week, eating those weird sandwiches, was gone. Vance wasn't talking, and Miss Winnie seemed absent. I felt like an intruder, interrupting their argument. But I didn't get the sense that Vance was exasperated, that he wanted me to leave so he could finish his argument. I wondered if he would have walked out had I not come in when I did.

"I don't think we'll work tomorrow," Miss Winnie said, bringing her cup of tea to her lips.

"Okay," I said. "I'm feeling a little bit sore, anyway. . . ."

"Vance will take you home," Miss Winnie said. She smiled, like she wanted to reassure me that everything was all right. "I'm glad you stayed with us last night."

"Thank you," I said again. I wished I could think of something better to say.

Vance stood up. "C'mon, let's go."

I followed Vance to the car. Again, he opened the door for me, but I think it was automatic more than polite.

This time, I didn't lead him through my school's Cherry Hills neighborhood, but directly to my house. I felt like saying something, like I should say something. Maybe I could ask him something about his nightclub dancing, but that idea made me feel guilty for eavesdropping.

"Will you be in class Wednesday?" I asked.

"I don't know."

"Oh, I forgot! Class will probably be canceled on Wednesday. There's an audition Wednesday night. Pacific Northwest Ballet School, I think. Are you going?"

For the first time today, he looked at me directly. "Are you?"

"Yes." I hadn't actually decided until that moment. Just the thought of walking into the big studio at the Colorado Ballet School—it filled me with fright. "Miss Winnie'll probably want you to go."

"What's the point?"

"I'm sure you could go to any dance program you wanted this summer," I said. "You'll probably get scholarships. Even at the School of American Ballet."

Vance shrugged, as if it all meant nothing to him.

I sighed, wishing it would be so easy for me. I'll bet Vance would be invited to stay on at whatever ballet school he went to this summer. He could be dancing in New York or San Francisco this time next year. "It's so much easier for guys—"

"Not really."

I blinked. I hadn't realized I'd spoken out loud. "What do you mean?"

Vance shook his head, like he would say no more on the subject. He parked the car in front of my house. "Here you are. At your mansion."

I grinned. "Yep. My mansion."

"Man, I thought you'd be rolling in cash."

"Well, I'm not."

"What about that school-uniform business?" He shut off the car engine, as if he expected us to sit and talk for a while. I was glad of that.

"My dad works at Lakeview. That's why I go to school there. I drove you past my school last week."

"What's he do?"

I looked at my house. The windows were dark. Maybe my parents weren't awake yet. "He's the head custodian."

"Oh . . ."

"It doesn't exactly make me a prima donna," I said. "I have a scholarship that pays for my ballet lessons."

He nodded, and it seemed as if he was really looking at me, really seeing me.

My stomach growled, almost as if it had untwisted itself and was now demanding food. "I should go. Thanks for the ride."

"No problem."

I trudged up the front walk to my house. I had to ring the doorbell because Gillian had my purse. Gillian . . . I pushed thoughts of the party from my head. I'd have to face her tomorrow, explain why I had disappeared. But I didn't want to think about that.

Dad answered the door, wearing his bathrobe. "Stephanie! Back so soon? How was the party?"

"Okay—" I brushed by him and went to the kitchen. Dad had the paper spread out on the table. I was annoyed; I had hoped to eat some breakfast alone. Nevertheless, I poured myself a big bowl of cereal and took it to the table.

Dad folded up the newspaper. "So tell me about the party."

"I'm kind of tired—can we talk about it later?" I ate quickly, wanting to finish my cereal so I could go to my room.

"I thought you'd be home a little later," Dad said. "You girls did leave the party at a decent hour, right?"

I nodded, my mouth full.

"And this Gillian girl, you like her?" Dad crossed his arms over his stomach and sat back in his chair. "Where's she from?"

"Atlanta."

"And what do her parents do?"

"I don't know."

"Her home must be something to see. What are her parents like?"

"I don't know. . . ."

"You didn't talk to them?" Dad said. "Didn't thank them for inviting you over?"

"I didn't go to her house!" Maybe Lisa Brown could lie easily to her parents, but I couldn't. I lowered my head to my cereal, waiting for the onslaught.

It didn't come, not at first.

I could feel Dad staring at me. "So where did you stay last night?" His voice was icy.

I spooned another mouthful of cereal, but my throat felt constricted, and I had to fight to swallow it.

Dad's voice was stern. "I'm expecting an answer!"

"I called Miss Winnie, and I stayed there. The party was stupid! I hated it! It was just a bunch of rich kids, and they made me feel awful! So I called Miss Winnie and went there. Are you happy now?"

I fled from the table.

"Stephanie, get back in here." Dad didn't shout. He didn't have to. But he used a voice that told me he expected me to do exactly as told.

So I turned around, my face on fire.

"Sit down."

I sat.

Dad folded his hands on the table and leaned toward me. "Now explain this to me."

"There's nothing to explain. I already told you what happened."

"Why didn't you call home?"

"Because I didn't feel like answering your questions, that's why! I knew you'd get on my case, but Miss Winnie, she . . . she . . ." I swallowed. "She listened to me. And then we practiced some ballet. Her nephew brought me home."

Dad raised his eyebrows. "He stayed over, too?"

"He lives there sometimes."

"Sometimes? What about other times?"

"I don't know. Why are you giving me the third degree? I'm glad I stayed over at Miss Winnie's! At least she understands me!" With that, I got up from the table and ran from the kitchen. This time, Dad didn't stop me.

twelve

Monday morning, Dad and I rode to school in silence. I crossed my arms and leaned against the door. I wasn't sorry for spending Friday night at Miss Winnie's, and I resented the notion that I should have been. All Dad said was, "Have a good day," before heading toward his basement office. I waited in the front lobby, watching the parking lot for Gillian's arrival. A few kids said hello to me as they sauntered in, all looking disturbingly similar in their navy blue uniforms.

Gillian drove up ten minutes before the first bell. I watched her step out of the car, her cardigan tied around her shoulders. In the front seat, Kelly Corbell fluffed out her dark hair. I was annoyed—I was hoping to talk to Gillian alone. I wondered if I should go out to meet her, but then I saw Bret Carlson pull his Jeep into the parking spot next to Gillian's. He jumped out and slung an arm around Gillian, and then Kelly hopped out of

Gillian's car and flung her arms around Bret's neck. I watched them greet one another: Kelly whispering something in Bret's ear, Bret ruffling Gillian's hair. The three of them approached the building, smiling about something. I was tempted to let them pass as they came through the heavy double doors, but I needed my purse and my dance bag.

"Gillian!" I called.

She looked around for a moment before she saw me. She said something to Kelly and Bret, and they continued on, up the staircase. I was glad they left.

Gillian came to me, wearing that bored-casual look that completely hid what she was thinking. "What's going on?"

"Sorry about Friday . . ." I had already thought up the lie I planned to tell her.

Gillian shrugged. "It was an okay party. Not that great."

"You looked like you were having a great time." I couldn't hide my hostility. After all, she did ignore me completely.

Either she didn't hear it or she pretended not to. "You just learn how to fake it, that's all. But you took off so quickly—"

"I had a migraine. Sometimes I get them after rehearsals. Sorry I didn't say anything, but I really needed to get out of there."

She seemed to buy it. "I've got your stuff in my car."

Finally! I followed her to the parking lot, where she retrieved my things.

"I met this guy," she was saying. "He goes to Centennial High. A senior. I was looking for you, and I ran into him. Bret knows him; I guess they hang out together sometimes. Anyway, he invited me to go to a basketball game with him this week."

"Cool," I said.

"He's pretty cute. Real dark-skinned, great body. He had a friend who was cute, too. Maybe you can come with us."

"Um . . . it depends . . ." I wasn't really sure why she was asking me, especially since we struck out last time. "I have an audition this week."

Gillian leaned against her car. "It was pretty cool. I'm in Snowflake City, and these two fine brothers show up. I was like, I've got to talk to them! Know what I mean? Hey, Lisa!" She waved at Lisa, who was standing in the doorway.

"It seems like you and Lisa and Kelly are good friends," I said. "I guess I don't know what you mean."

"I guess you wouldn't, would you, Miss Ballerina?"

"Well, you're one to talk, Miss Lakeview Country Day!" The words poured out like venom. I couldn't help it.

Gillian's mouth fell open, and I turned around and left her. I didn't need anyone judging me, least of all Gillian Sporer!

She didn't say anything to me in study hall. She sat huddled together with Lisa and Kelly as usual, but every now and then she'd look over at me, almost like she wanted to come talk to me. But she didn't. I had other things on my mind, anyway. Mainly, the Pacific Northwest Ballet School audition. Bridget and I could talk of nothing else at lunch. Bridget was terrified. She'd never been to a major audition before. Neither had I. I was scared, too.

On Wednesday, instead of taking us to the studio, Bridget's mother drove us downtown to the Colorado Ballet Academy. We entered the building and made our way to the dressing room. It seemed as if every bit of floor space was taken by long-legged girls with their hair in buns. Hairspray misted on me as

Bridget and I found a tiny space to change amid the mass of audition hopefuls. It seemed like every serious dance student in Denver was in this room. Bridget's face was ghost-white with fear.

"Relax," I whispered to her. "It'll be just like taking class."

But I was nervous, too, as I looked around the room. I couldn't help but notice I was the only black girl there. I remembered Gillian making a dot on a blank sheet of paper in study hall. That's how I felt right now amid all the super-thin, confident-looking girls. Freshly peeled apple. An image of George Balanchine's description of a ballerina's ideal skin tone came to me then. I saw only a few girls who fit that exact description. *But the rest could, with makeup,* my ugly voice said, *and no amount of makeup's ever going to liken you to a freshly peeled apple.*

Grabbing my pointe shoes, I waited for Bridget, and we left the dressing room together. The hallways and the front lobby were just as crowded: girls stretched splay-legged on the floor, did *pliés* holding on to doorframes and the edges of chairs, sat whispering in groups. I held my head high, trying to look as confident as possible. Bridget cowered beside me, her scrawny shoulders hunched over. I looked through the crowd for a familiar face as we stood in line waiting to sign in and receive the numbers we would pin onto our leotards. I knew Camilla and Ursula weren't coming.

"No way!" Camilla had said yesterday in ballet class. "Why would I want to spend the summer in Seattle, anyway? It rains all the time!" Ursula had said she wasn't feeling well, but I knew she felt too insecure to come.

"Look, there's Anna!" Bridget pointed to a corner of the hallway, where Anna Gritschuk was putting up her hair. She raised her hand as if to wave, then lowered it, like she'd changed her mind.

Anna saw us and offered a little smile. I motioned in front of me, and she came to stand with us. Her face looked even paler than usual, but she seemed grateful to see us. "I have not been to an audition like this before."

Bridget looked at her without speaking.

"It shouldn't be too bad," I said. "It'll just be a ballet class."

"Have you been to this ballet program?" Anna asked.

"No. I went to a camp in Aspen the last few years," I said. "I auditioned by video the first time, and then they kept inviting me back. This is my first real audition, too."

Anna nodded, looking as if she was glad to hear it. "Back in Kiev, I just took class. Nothing serious."

"Really?" Bridget said.

"South Metropolitan is a much better school. Our studio—it was so old. The floor gave us all, what do you call it? The pain in the leg?"

"Shin splints?" I said when she pointed to her shins.

"Yes. Our teacher, she was very bad."

This was the most I'd ever heard Anna say at one time. I was surprised—I would have thought she came from one of those Soviet-style dance factories where everyone was perfectly proportioned and severe-looking. But more than anything, I was surprised at how friendly she sounded.

My eye caught a brightly colored turban, and I wanted to cheer. "Be right back!" I said and ran to Miss Winnie, who entered the building holding Vance's arm.

She wore green this time: shining like an emerald in a flowing dress. A lot of heads turned as she entered the lobby. Who could help but notice her? Her arms enveloped me.

"I'm so glad to see you!" I said, feeling better immediately. I turned to Vance, who stood by the door as if he wanted to leave

"Hi," I said.

"What's up?" His voice was a monotone.

"Go get ready!" Miss Winnie waved him off, then took both my hands in hers. "Are you nervous?"

"Yeah. Everyone looks like a perfect dancer."

"No one's perfect," Miss Winnie said. "Just do your best."

She motioned for me to rejoin the line, which I did. Anna and Bridget were both looking at Miss Winnie as she took a seat. A lot of my anxiety dissipated. Just knowing she was here made everything better.

"She's really into ballet, isn't she?" Bridget said.

"I go to her house on Sundays, and she works with Vance and me." It made me feel important, saying that. Bridget and Anna both seemed impressed.

I pinned number 46 to my leotard. Bridget was 47, Anna, 48. Vance, when he appeared in the studio, was number 63. I had saved him a place at one of the center barres.

The class was led by a tall, sallow-faced man with a whiny voice. Two women sat on folding chairs, their faces expressionless, audition forms piled on top of clipboards. I stood as straight and tall as possible, executing the barre combinations as cleanly and correctly as I could. I worked hard; a film of sweat covered my skin after the opening *plié* combination. More than eighty dancers were packed in the studio. I wondered how two women could judge us all.

In center floor, it became easy to see how. During barre, I had been so focused on my technique that I wasn't paying attention to the other dancers in the room. During the first center-floor exercise, a simple *tendu* combination, I noticed that the judges looked at only a few dancers in each group. Everyone else was invisible. And as I performed my *tendus,* I got the sinking feeling that no one was watching me.

Everyone watched Vance. He made a lot of mistakes, but his talent was impossible to ignore. I watched one of the judges staring at him as he performed the *adagio,* her eyes never straying from him during the entire exercise. She sat with her chin in her hand, her eyes narrowed at Vance. And Bridget was in Vance's group. I watched her grit her teeth as she lifted her leg as high as she could, although no one paid any attention to her efforts.

The judges watched Anna, though. I saw both of them look at Anna as she did *pirouettes,* then scribble something on their forms.

I turned, I jumped, I leaped, as hard and as high and as fast as I could, but by the end of the audition, I just wanted to cry. No one had looked at me. I may as well not even have been there. At the end of the class, we were told we'd be notified of our acceptance or rejection in a month.

Bridget looked as dejected as I felt as we left the studio, sweat trailing down our foreheads and backs, suctioning our leotards to our skin. "So much for that," she said.

Anna pointed into the studio. "Look, they're talking to Vance." One of the judges had stopped Vance on his way out.

"It's so much easier for boys!" Bridget wailed. There were five boys at the audition. Vance was the only one I thought was any good, but I wouldn't have been surprised if all five of them got invited to the school. I imagined this scene taking place in cities all over the country. Auditions crowded with girls, only a few making the cut. My ugly voice surfaced. *What makes you think you could be one of them?*

Miss Winnie stood up as we approached. "How did it go, girls?"

"Terrible," Bridget said, the only one who replied. I gave a shrug. Miss Winnie nodded, looking at me sympathetically. But she said nothing.

"They really liked Vance, though," I said. "He's in there talking with them now."

Vance walked out of the studio with a towel around his shoulders.

"What'd they say?" I asked him.

He looked noncommittal. "They asked me what my plans were for the summer. I told them I didn't know."

"They want you," Bridget said.

Vance didn't answer.

Bridget looked at me. "Mom's gonna be here soon. We'd better get changed."

"I'll see you tomorrow at rehearsal," Anna said to me.

Rehearsal. Oh yes. *Sleeping Beauty.* Madame Caroline had called a rehearsal for me, Anna, and Vance before class.

"See you," I echoed before saying good-bye to Vance and Miss Winnie. Maybe Camilla was right. Maybe it rained too much in Seattle, anyway.

thirteen

"One more time," Miss Winnie said on Sunday. I wiped away the sweat that stung my eyes and took my place in the center of the studio. The muscles in my legs ached, my feet throbbed, and my breathing was ragged, but I summoned the energy to dance one more time as the music began. Rising onto pointe, I turned to Vance and lifted my arms. His movements mirrored mine; we danced apart as we danced together, executing the same steps, spinning around each other until I leaped toward him and he caught me at the waist, lifting me over his head as I opened my arms wide, my head lifted to the sky. He lowered me—not as gently as he should have; the descent would improve with more practice—and then I leaned against him, my arms wrapped around his neck, my leg in a low *arabesque*. I felt the warmth of his chest through his tank top, which was transparent with sweat. But I figured I must be nearly as gross to touch as he was, as hard as we'd been working. Anyway, it wasn't gross. Not really.

The music stopped, and I moved away from Vance. Miss Winnie's face glowed with her pleasure. "It's going to be beautiful," she said. "Absolutely beautiful."

I was smiling. I wanted to open my arms wide and embrace them both for letting me be a part of this, giving me the chance to feel so incredible.

Vance and I collapsed onto the floor as Miss Winnie left to prepare lunch.

"I thought I was going to drop dead halfway through that last run-through." I was so out of breath, I could barely talk. "But you know what? I didn't care! Nothing could have made me stop dancing."

Vance lay on his back, his chest heaving up and down as he breathed deeply. "I don't remember the last time I was so worn out."

"Me neither." We'd been working for two hours straight without a break, putting together Miss Winnie's pas de deux. And now it was actually starting to feel like something substantial.

"I think we're good together," I said. Vance rolled onto his side, and I added quickly, "Dancing, I mean."

"Maybe."

I thought of Vance and Anna, the rehearsal for *Sleeping Beauty* the three of us had had together this week. In Act 2, the Prince shows up at Sleeping Beauty's castle, and the Lilac Fairy shows him a vision of the Princess Aurora, who's been asleep inside the castle for a hundred years. During the vision scene, the Prince, the Princess Aurora, and the Lilac Fairy dance a pas de trois, which we began to rehearse on Thursday. The Lilac Fairy doesn't dance a whole lot; she spends most of her time standing to the side as the Prince chases a fleeting vision of the Princess. I remembered Madame Caroline's instructing me to take Vance's hand and lead him to Anna, then stand aside as he lifts her into the air. From my pose, I watched Vance try to embrace Anna as she ran away. He would catch her, dance with her briefly, and then she would escape. I placed myself between them, miming to Vance that this was only a vision, that the Princess lay asleep inside. And even in her faded, stretched-out practice leotard, Anna looked like a vision. It wasn't jealousy I felt as she lifted her leg high to the side, holding Vance's hand, then turning to *arabesque* and dipping into a *penchée.* It was amazement, awe, and even sadness. I remembered thinking, Could I ever look like that? She danced as if she were made of air. At one point she stood behind me with her hand on my shoulder, and I actually became her partner, promenading her in a slow circle. The pressure of her hand on my shoulder was almost imperceptible. And I stood to the side, feeling almost like an intruder every time I led Vance away from Anna.

"Where are you?" Vance broke the silence.

"I was thinking about *Sleeping Beauty.*"

"Still mad that you're not Sleeping Beauty?"

I stared at the ceiling. "What makes you think I was?"

"I have eyes."

I sat up now, growing defensive. "What does that mean?"

"Look, you told me yourself you've been at that school forever. And then Anna shows up from out of nowhere and she gets the lead. You're telling me that doesn't piss you off?"

"Anna's a great dancer. You should know, you've had all those rehearsals with her!"

Vance was looking at me strangely. Maybe it was pity,

maybe it was sympathy, I wasn't sure. But it made me uncomfortable all the same.

"Besides," I said. "Who knows if I even could have danced the role anyway. Maybe I'm not good enough for it."

Now Vance sat up. "You don't believe that, do you?"

I shrugged.

"Well, you shouldn't believe it."

I looked at him. "You really think I'm good?"

Vance smiled in a really sweet way. But the smile disappeared quickly and his usual sardonic expression returned. "Well, we're tearing up this pas de deux, don't you think?"

He got up and strode out of the studio.

When I got to the kitchen, Miss Winnie was setting a large bowl of salad on the table.

Vance wrinkled his nose. "Why can't we just order a pizza?"

Miss Winnie motioned for him to set the table. "You children need nutrients. Vitamins. Besides, I have a surprise for you."

"Yeah?" Vance shoveled a forkful of salad into his mouth. He grimaced with distaste as he chewed. I stifled a giggle.

"We're going to see the Dance Theatre of Harlem on Wednesday night."

"The Dance Theatre of Harlem?" I shrieked. I had seen advertisements in December about their appearance, but the tickets were so expensive, I knew I couldn't possibly go.

"I got tickets," she said.

"But . . . they're so expensive!"

Miss Winnie waved a hand dismissively. "It's my pleasure, child." She smiled, looking from me to Vance. "And who else do I have to spend my money on?"

"Oh my goodness!" I thought I would stop breathing. "Oh my goodness!"

"And it's important for both of you to see the company, to see the level of dancing a professional career demands," Miss Winnie went on, "the level of dancing I expect to see from both of you someday."

Vance set down his fork and crossed his arms. He scowled at the table, and for one irritated moment I wondered why he had to have such an attitude about everything. But the moment passed as the realization sunk in. The Dance Theatre of Harlem! I was actually going to see the Dance Theatre of Harlem!

"Thank you so much!" I wished I could put into words everything I was feeling.

Miss Winnie was smiling. "I'll bet Arthur Mitchell will let you two take class with the company if I ask him."

My pulse quickened. "But I—I'm not—"

"Nonsense." Miss Winnie cut me off. "Besides, I've known Arthur for a long time."

Class with the company. I felt faint at the thought of it. What if I made an enormous fool of myself? What if they laughed me out of the studio?

"No need to look so nervous, dear." My fears must have been written all over my face, because Miss Winnie smiled in a reassuring way. "It would be a wonderful experience for you."

"Do we have any choice in the matter?" Vance said this under his breath, but it was loud enough for me and Miss Winnie to hear.

"It will be a wonderful experience for both of you," Miss Winnie said firmly, like she was refusing to pay attention to any negativity.

I couldn't pay attention to Vance's attitude, either. "I just—I can't believe it! I can't—" I was repeating myself, I know it. But Miss Winnie looked happy, as happy as I felt.

Vance drove me home not long after lunch. All I could talk about was the Dance Theatre of Harlem. "Could you imagine taking class with them?" I kept saying. "It'll be the most incredible thing I've ever done in my life!"

Vance said nothing.

"Oh come on, don't tell me you're not excited, too!"

He pulled into a McDonald's near my house. "You hungry?"

I stared at the Golden Arches in disbelief. "But we just ate."

"Rabbit food. And you hardly ate anything, carrying on about Dance Theatre of Harlem."

He was right. I'd hardly eaten at all.

Vance grinned. "C'mon. You look like you could use a Big Mac."

The thought of a Big Mac made my stomach turn. "So you want me to walk into company class in front of Arthur Mitchell on Wednesday looking like a blimp?"

"Oh come on, one meal at McDonald's isn't gonna make you fat! Come on . . ." He smiled teasingly. "You know you want it!"

I laughed. "Now you sound like a peer-pressure-avoidance commercial. I feel like I should just say no."

Vance laughed with me. "You're telling me that if I go through the drive-through and get an Extra Value meal, you won't get one with me? You'll just sit there watching me stuff my face?"

I thought for a moment. When was the last time I had fast food anyway?

He must've sensed my considering the prospect, because he patted me on the back and said, "That's my girl!"

He pulled into the drive-through and I sat blushing as he ordered a Big Mac Value meal. I told him to make mine a Happy Meal. "Happy Meal?" he repeated, but I held firm.

So we sat in the parking lot, him eating a Big Mac, me eating a cheeseburger and small fries. And I had to admit, those French fries tasted awfully good. Maybe I'd regret it tomorrow, but right then, I was just enjoying myself. I tried not to think about how Vance had said, "That's my girl." Anyway, he meant it in jest. I knew that. But why that choice of words? And what would it be like to be his—

Stop it! I told myself and tried to concentrate on my French fries.

"Isn't this better than some old salad?" Vance looked as if he was enjoying his food, too.

"How often do you eat this stuff?"

"Not much. If Miss Winnie saw me, she'd have a fit!"

"What about your mother?"

Vance was silent a moment before he spoke. "I don't suppose it matters too much what I do. To her, I mean. What're you gonna do with the prize, anyway?"

"Prize?" I'd forgotten that Happy Meals come with toy prizes. I reached into the bottom of the box and pulled out a Hot Wheels car.

"Ferrari," Vance said with approval.

I spun its wheels. "It's probably the only Ferrari I'll ever own."

"Maybe you'll be a badass ballerina some day."

"Even still, I don't think I could afford a Ferrari."

Vance shrugged and motioned for me to give him my trash.

"Oh well." He left the car to dump the trash into a bin. The car smelled like French fries now.

I lowered the windows as Vance returned. "We should air out the car."

"You're right." He pulled out of the parking lot.

I was sorry when he reached my house. "Thanks for lunch," I said. He had paid, anyway. Come to think of it, this was the first time a guy had ever bought me lunch. I wanted to giggle at that thought, but luckily, I didn't.

"See you Wednesday," he said.

Wednesday. The thought was exhilarating. I couldn't remember ever having had so much to look forward to before today.

fourteen

Mom and Dad were watching TV in the den when I came in. I treaded as softly as I could, hoping they wouldn't notice me. But Dad called, "Stephanie?"

I sighed, exasperated, and stood in the den's entryway. Mom and Dad were both in their bathrobes. The TV screen reflected against Mom's glasses. I glanced around the den, at the worn brown sofa, the frayed carpet. Mom had bought new lamps for the end tables last week; the pleated white lampshades still wore their protective plastic covering.

"Don't forget to vacuum the stairs today," Dad said.

I rocked on my heels, impatient. "Okay. Is that all?"

"Did you have a good time at your class?" Mom asked.

I was backing out of the den as I spoke. "Yeah, it was fine."

"Stephanie!" Dad sat up a little, and I remained in the doorway. I wished he would just say what he wanted so I could go. "I thought we'd go see a movie tonight. The three of us."

"Can't. I have homework."

Dad looked disappointed, but he nodded. "Well, I guess you should get to it, then."

"Okay." Finally! I went downstairs to my room and shut the door. Flinging myself on the bed, I stared at the ceiling. Thinking about the Dance Theatre of Harlem brought a smile to my face. I was going to see the company, and maybe I'd even take class with them! I imagined myself as a member of the company, traveling all over the world, performing in beautiful theaters, hearing the applause every night. My life would be exciting, full of adventure. From my bedroom window, I could see down our street, a row of houses lined up like neat little dominoes. The sight was dissatisfying. I mean, when do people decide that they're just going to be ordinary? That they're going to go to work, come home, maybe go out to eat or to a movie now and then, be one of the faceless nobodies in a crowd? Miss Winnie, she was someone people noticed. Maybe she didn't have the career she'd wanted, but she still could be close to what she loved. That's what's important, I think. Doing something you love, not slaving away at some job. And how can you be passionate about cleaning up after rich brats or pushing around paper in a factory office?

I rolled over on my side and put my head in my hands. I'd have to tell my parents about the Dance Theatre of Harlem. If I took company class, it'd mean I'd have to miss school. Well, Mom and Dad better not give me any trouble about it! I started thinking of arguments in advance. I hadn't missed a day of school this semester; I was all caught up in my schoolwork. And how could they object to my seeing an all-black classical ballet company? Dad was the one going off about my not having a chance to make it in ballet. This could show him!

I decided to confront them now, while I was thinking about it. I marched upstairs to the den. Mom and Dad hadn't moved from their places on the couch. "Miss Winnie invited me to go to see the Dance Theatre of Harlem on Wednesday night."

Mom and Dad looked up.

"She's treating me and her nephew. It's at the Buell Theatre downtown. She got tickets for all three of us. And she's even gonna see if we can take class with the company on Wednesday, too."

"Oh?" Mom said, but Dad said, "Wait a minute, back up a minute. Now, what is this?"

I sighed, impatient. "The Dance Theatre of Harlem. The all-black ballet company! They're coming to town, and Miss Winnie got tickets for us!"

"How much do these tickets cost?" Dad asked.

I already said that, I wanted to exclaim, but I restrained myself. "Miss Winnie bought them! She wants us to see the company. And we might even get to take class with them. Don't you see what a great opportunity this is for me?"

Mom and Dad looked at each other, and they didn't look happy. That made me angry, but I bit my lip to avoid lashing out.

"That's very generous of her," Mom said, but she sounded sort of noncommittal, as if she was just being polite. Mom and Dad looked at each other again, then Mom turned to me.

"Stephanie." Her voice was really low, which I took as a warning. Mom always speaks in a soft voice when she says something that'll make me mad. "Your father and I were wondering if you're spending too much time with—"

"Oh no!" I clamped my hands over my ears and shut my eyes tightly. I opened my eyes to see them both looking at me in that "concerned-parent" way. It's the I'm-trying-to-be-patient look that I absolutely hate.

Mom didn't raise her voice. "You spend the night at her house without telling us, these Sunday sessions are getting longer and longer, and now she wants to take you to a concert—"

"You just don't want me to dance, and you're mad that I've found someone who actually believes in me!" I shot back. "Why are you trying to ruin this for me? Why?" I was near tears.

"Stephanie." Dad was taking deep breaths, like he was trying not to lose his patience. "Aren't you being a little dramatic here?"

"You're the ones being dramatic, not me!" I was shouting now.

Mom and Dad looked at each other again.

"Why can't you just be happy for me? It's not like I'm going out doing drugs or sneaking out! It's not like I don't get good grades at school! But you don't even care!" I fled to my room then, my eyes blurry with tears, and rage like a ball of fire in my chest. Well, I wasn't asking their permission to go. I was going, and that was all there was to it!

I threw myself on my bed and wiped at my tears with my blanket. Right then I wanted to be at Miss Winnie's house, lying in that big canopied bed. Vance said he lived with Miss Winnie when he didn't want to live at home. Oh, I wished I could do the same! Miss Winnie wouldn't bug me like my parents. She wouldn't put on that stupid I'm-so-concerned look anytime I talked about ballet. She would ask me how class went and, when I told her, would understand what I was talking about. I could even tell her about school and she'd understand! Vance was lucky to have her for an aunt.

I heard a soft tapping at my door. Go away, I wanted to shout, but I didn't. I said nothing. The door opened, and, to my surprise, both Mom and Dad came into my room. Dad stood in the doorway while Mom sat on the edge of my bed. She touched my forehead, and I sat stiffly, looking from one to the other.

I wiped my face and said, "I'll go vacuum the stairs."

"The stairs can wait," Dad said. He didn't look angry. In fact, he looked sad. Sad and tired. But what did he have to be sad about?

"Then what?" I sounded rude, but I couldn't help it.

"What time is the show?" Mom asked.

"Eight. Do you want Miss Winnie to call you with the details?" My voice was flat.

"Yes, I'd like to hear from her," Mom said.

"If you took a ballet class with this dance troupe, when would it be?" Dad asked.

"During the day sometime. But I haven't missed school at all this semester! I think this is a good excuse. Besides, how many times does the—"

"Stephanie." Dad cut me off and smiled gently. "I suppose one day off won't hurt."

I wiped my face again. "I can go?" What a relief!

"We're not ogres, Stephanie," Dad said. "We just want what's best for you."

I nodded a little. But I know what's best for me, better than you, I wanted to say. But why risk antagonizing them again?

Mom and Dad went back upstairs, and I began to plan for Wednesday. I had a black dress I'd only worn once; it was the nicest dress I owned. And then for class, what would I wear? My best leotard . . . my head was spinning with all of my plans.

On Monday morning, during study hall, I was still trying to decide what I would wear, how I would fix my hair. After all, this would also be the first time Vance had seen me in anything other than practice clothes and my stupid school uniform. I wasn't paying any attention to Kelly, Lisa, and Gillian and their business. Seeing them huddled up in their usual fashion, all I could think was how I had much better things to do than be bothered with them. I couldn't wait to tell Bridget at lunch about the Dance Theatre of Harlem! She would be excited for me.

Gillian came to talk to me near the end of study hall. "Hey, Steph," she said, like we were great friends and hung out every day. She sat in the desk next to mine.

I didn't answer. I just folded my arms across my chest and waited to hear what she wanted from me.

"Remember how I told you about those two guys from Centennial? They're gonna meet me here after school today. I wondered if you wanted to meet Clay."

"Clay?"

"Frankie, he's the guy I like. Clay's his friend. I went to a club with them Saturday night. It was pretty cool." Gillian flipped her hair over one shoulder. It was irritating, the way she kept flipping her hair around.

"Anyway, we saw that guy you were dancing with; what's his name?"

"Vance?" Now I leaned toward her, a flush heating my face.

"Yeah, he was in a dance contest with some other guys. They were pretty good. I guess Clay and Frankie know him from school or something."

"What'd they say about him?" My heart was pounding, but I tried to keep my face as blank as possible.

"They said he's a real player. I know that girl Camilla said he was taken, but I guess he's, like, with a different girl every week."

I felt sick, as if someone had punched me in the stomach. I couldn't speak.

"Frankie and Clay, they don't like him too much. They think he's stuck on himself." Gillian laughed now. "Man, did they laugh when I said I saw him at your ballet studio! It'll be funny to see if they say anything to him about it."

I wanted to put my head on the desk and bury my face. I wanted Gillian to leave. But she didn't leave. Instead, she said, "So how about coming out to meet Frankie and Clay with me. I told them about you."

What did she know about me, anyway? "What did you say?"

She twirled a lock of hair around her finger. "I just said you were pretty and you were a dancer." She leaned toward me. "I also said I thought you could loosen up a little."

I was getting angry. "What does that mean?"

"Don't lose your temper! Why do you take everything so seriously?" Gillian leaned back in her seat. "All I meant is that I think we could have a lot of fun with these guys if you'd just lighten up a little! I had fun with them Saturday night."

I could hardly think straight. All I kept hearing was her saying Vance was a player. Come on, it's not like you have anything going with him, I told myself. And when he said, That's my girl, maybe that's just how he talks. Besides, he did go out with Camilla, didn't he?

Gillian kept going on about the guys, as if she hadn't noticed my silence. "And you should see Frankie's wheels! He's got a Beemer, but he's not like all these spoiled brats at this school. He and Clay were joking around at Kelly's party, saying how their houses could fit inside Kelly's kitchen. And he dresses real sharp—"

"I have ballet after school."

Gillian blinked, like she lost her train of thought. She lowered her head, like she was disappointed. When she looked up, her casual-bored look had returned. "See you around, then."

She got up and went back over to Lisa and Kelly. Now I did put my elbows on my desk and my face in my hands. I wanted to be sick to my stomach. So maybe Vance was just a jerk like that Bret Carlson. But then why was he being nice to me? And when we danced together, it was like there was really something there between us. I thought of all my plans for Wednesday. Oh, I'd fix myself up all right! I looked over at Gillian, remembering how she'd said she'd show me how to dress up, look older. And I was mad at myself for blowing her off.

She looked deep in conversation with Kelly and Lisa, but I summoned my nerve and approached her. After all, she had used me before with that slumber party business; I could use her, too!

"Gillian," I said loudly as I approached their group. Lisa looked up, like she was surprised to see me. But I ignored them, focusing on Gillian.

I tried to mirror her bored-casual look. "I can't meet those guys today, but I'd really like to meet them sometime soon. Can we talk?"

"Okay." Gillian got up, and we went back to my desk. She sat on the edge of it.

"I'm going out with someone on Wednesday. I was wondering if you could help me fix up, you know?"

She smiled. "Who is it?"

"A guy I know . . . from the Colorado Ballet," I said, so she wouldn't get suspicious. "The Dance Theatre of Harlem's coming to town, and we're gonna see them."

"For real? I saw them in Atlanta last year."

"I'm gonna take class with them, too."

Gillian looked impressed. "Cool. Tell you what. What about after your ballet class today? We could go to your house—"

My neck tightened at that thought. No way would I bring Gillian to my house! "It might be too late. I have a rehearsal—"

"Then tomorrow in study hall. We'll do your makeup then," Gillian said. She looked confident. She went back to Lisa and Kelly, and I started thinking that maybe Gillian wasn't so stuck-up after all.

fifteen

Wednesday morning, I sat waiting by the door, looking out the window in nervous anticipation. Under my jeans and sweatshirt, I wore my best leotard, a dark green camisole. At ten o'clock, a car honked out front. My heart leaped as I picked up my dance bag and hurried out the door. Miss Winnie's burgundy sedan was in the driveway, with Vance at the wheel. Sunglasses hid his eyes.

Miss Winnie turned to smile at me as I slid into the back seat. She wore her most elaborate get-up yet: a multicolored turban and a dress that looked like kente cloth. She looked like an African goddess. "Are you ready for class?" she asked.

"I've been stretching all morning," I said as Vance pulled out of my driveway. He nodded to me as I buckled my seat belt. I nodded back. I could see his face in the rearview mirror as he drove, but the black sunglasses hid his expression. Soft classical music was on the radio, and the pounding in my heart intensified as the Denver skyline loomed before me.

"Where will class take place?" I asked.

"On the stage," Miss Winnie said. "Have you ever been on the Buell stage before?"

"I have," I said. "I was a clown in the *Nutcracker* for two years, and then a toy soldier for two years before that."

Vance's head tilted upward as he looked at me in the mirror.

"It was a lot of fun," I said. The Colorado Ballet uses children from all of its affiliated schools in its *Nutcracker,* but my last time on that big stage had been when I was twelve.

We were approaching Denver's huge performing arts complex, and I thought I was going to faint. It's just a class, I tried to tell myself. In many ways, classes are the same everywhere, at least in format. You always begin at the barre, always with *pliés.* But was I ready to take a class with a professional company?

Vance parked the car, and my hands shook as I opened the door. I tried to take slow, deep breaths as we entered the lobby of the empty theater. Tonight, thousands of people in fancy clothes would be milling about, sipping wine. And someday, I could really dance on stages like this, not just as a child extra in *The Nutcracker.*

Entering the auditorium, I saw portable barres set out on stage and dancers standing and sitting on stage in small clusters. I glanced at Vance, but he seemed nonchalant. He immediately took off his jacket, revealing his standard tank top and sweats outfit. Looking at the stage, I realized he would blend in better than I would. The dancers all wore heavy leg warmers, sweaters, multicolored scarves, torn sweatpants. Madame Caroline would never let us take class wearing so much junk. I took off my jeans and shirt, wishing I had brought some leg warmers with me. I wanted to turn and run out. But Miss Winnie had me by the arm and was leading me up toward the stage.

Up close, the dancers were even more imposing-looking. Some looked young, late teens even, but I couldn't tell how old most of them were. Seeing all of them made me realize that black was not a color but a spectrum: cinnamon brown, walnut brown, café au lait, raisin; there were more hues present than I could label. Here and there I saw a dancer who looked Hispanic. All of the women wore pointe shoes dyed to match their skin tone. I immediately felt out of place as I laced on my pink pointe shoes. My shoes might as well have been neon green, they stood out so much. But no one really paid Vance or me any attention. A few of the dancers glanced our way, then turned back to whatever they were doing. One or two of them even smiled at us. I couldn't get any sense of what they thought of Vance's and my being there. Maybe people came to take class with them all the time. The generic work lights overhead made my face feel uncomfortably warm. It would be strange taking class on a stage and without mirrors, but maybe it'd be even scarier if I could see myself.

A very elegant-looking man stood in a corner, talking with a female dancer. I elbowed Vance. "That's Arthur Mitchell!" I whispered as Miss Winnie left us to glide across the stage toward him. I watched them embrace. I couldn't believe it. I was standing there, looking at a true dance pioneer. This was the man who had integrated the New York City Ballet, and I was standing on the same stage as him! I looked at Vance, but he didn't speak. Perspiration gleamed on his forehead. He was nervous, too.

Miss Winnie waved us over. My feet moved toward her, but they felt like they were made of wood. I had a smile on my face, an anxious smile that hurt my cheeks.

Arthur Mitchell was a handsome man; he had a sort of ageless look about him. He shook my hand firmly and looked me in the eye. He told us he was glad we were joining the class today. He spoke quickly, like a busy person making time for you; but at the same time, he spoke with a casual nonchalance, almost as if we took class with his company every day. Miss Winnie motioned for us to take places at the barre as the company began to fill the stage. I reluctantly followed Vance to the center-stage barre. My nerves would have led me to a place in the back corner of the stage, but I had to remember that I was here to be seen, not to hide. Vance and I were immediately sandwiched between two tall men from the company, both dark-skinned, both wearing ratty ballet shoes over the most incredibly arched feet I had ever seen up-close.

Arthur Mitchell didn't teach class. A woman, I didn't catch her name, clapped her hands to bring the class to order. Miss Winnie sat in the first row of the auditorium watching us.

The class began very slowly, with us facing the barre, rolling through the feet to *relevé* on full pointe, then rolling down again. The class gained in speed and momentum with each exercise. I don't think I've ever done so many *tendus* at one time in my life. Halfway through barre I was weary from the mental exertion as much as the physical. I made lots of mistakes. So did Vance. But I didn't make a fool of myself; I could keep up with the combinations. I was happy when I got two corrections during barre. That meant the teacher was watching me, that I wasn't being ignored.

The dancers were all so amazingly good! They had such incredible extensions and jumps and turns. I was happy when I did a clean quadruple *pirouette* in center floor, wobbling only the tiniest bit on the landing.

"Nice," the teacher nodded and said.

Vance looked at me and grinned.

After class, my mind and body were numb from exhaustion. Vance slung an arm around my shoulders, breathing heavily. "Not bad. What do you think?"

"I don't know," I said. As tired as I was, I felt tranquil, purified. I had an intuitive feeling that I belonged here. No, that I *could* belong here. I could never join the company now; my technique wasn't good enough yet. But someday?

Miss Winnie came onto the stage arm in arm with Arthur Mitchell.

He wore a big smile as he looked from me to Vance. I spoke first, thanking him again in a shaky voice for letting me take class. To my surprise, he asked me to take off my pointe shoes so he could see my feet. I glanced at Miss Winnie, who nodded and smiled. I took off my shoes and wiggled my toes. Mr. Mitchell sat on the floor and took one of my feet in his hands. Vance held me steady as Mr. Mitchell flexed and pointed my foot, his brow furrowed. He then stood up and motioned for me to stand up straight. Very gently, but firmly, he lifted my leg to the side. I tried to relax as he pushed my leg higher and higher. I could feel the pressure of Vance's fingertips on my waist, which allowed me to keep my balance. Mr. Mitchell lifted my leg until my foot was pointed toward the ceiling. He then lowered my leg, looking, at least to me, satisfied. He told me to continue working on improving the articulation of my feet and legs, then he examined Vance's legs and feet and told him the same thing. He stood up, smiled at us one more time, and told us to come to New York in a year and take class with the company again.

Miss Winnie was positively beaming as she hugged both Vance and me close. "I'm so proud of you both," she said. And right then, I knew I would do anything to please her, to make her proud of me.

Vance drove me home. I was exhausted, but my brain just wouldn't slow down. I couldn't wait to tell the girls at the studio about the class! I especially wanted Madame Caroline to overhear my saying how Arthur Mitchell told me I did nice work!

So I went ahead and started getting ready for the performance tonight. Yesterday during study hall, Gillian had shown me how to do my makeup. Lisa and Kelly had helped. Gillian had actually pulled a lighted makeup mirror out of her book bag, and the three of them fussed around me, trying out different shades of lipstick and blush. It was embarrassing more than anything, especially with the other kids in the class looking on curiously.

I didn't think I looked very different with makeup on. Some women, I've noticed, look like completely different people with and without makeup. There was a day at school a few weeks ago when I passed Lisa Brown in the hallway and I almost didn't recognize her. It was early in the morning; her face without makeup looked wan and pasty. As I looked in the mirror, I frowned a little. I looked pretty much the same. My eyes seemed a little bigger with eyeliner, but that was it. So much for looking older. Then again, maybe I hadn't put on my makeup exactly the way Gillian had told me.

I put on my nicest dress, a short black sheath with thin straps. Every fashion magazine I've ever read has said that every girl should own a little black dress. So that's what I had asked for for Christmas. Instead of pulling my hair up into its usual bun, I brushed it out so that it hung loosely around my neck. I inspected myself in my full-length mirror. Not bad. I don't think anyone would ever put me on the cover of a magazine, but I thought I looked nice. For a blushing moment I wondered what Vance would think. This would be the first time he'd ever seen me dressed up.

I was glad my parents weren't home from work yet; I wouldn't want them fussing over me. When the doorbell rang, my pulse immediately quickened. I ran out of the room and up the stairs before realizing I had forgotten my purse. I turned quickly, practically tripping down the stairs. I snatched my purse, then ran upstairs to the door.

A peek through the peephole showed Vance standing on the other side. He looked—wow—he looked really, really good. His black slacks had a sharp crease. Over them he wore a white shirt with a black blazer. No tie, but he didn't seem like the tie type anyway. The tips of his black shoes gleamed from beneath his pants. I took a deep breath before opening the door.

He looked at me for a moment, but I couldn't read any response from his quick appraisal. When he smiled a little, I felt myself smiling back. "C'mon," he said and I followed him out to the car.

Magical would be the best word to describe the show. The Dance Theatre of Harlem performed a mix of classical and contemporary works, including George Balanchine's *Serenade,* which featured girls in gorgeous long blue tutus. Miss Winnie looked rapt as she watched, her eyes glistening. Vance, slumped in his seat on my other side, watched silently, without Miss Winnie's passionate involvement or my own awe and longing. During intermission, she bought us cappuccinos and a glass of white wine for herself. "It's so wonderful," she kept saying, "so wonderful." But she almost seemed sad as she said it, as if she wished she were the one on stage.

"What'd you think, Vance?" I asked him as he gingerly sipped his drink.

"It's okay," he said, setting his drink down. He didn't pick it up again.

"Just okay?" I exclaimed, but Miss Winnie waved him off.

"That's just Vance. Won't get excited for anything." Miss Winnie put a gentle arm around my shoulder. "Someday, I'll be sitting in the audience watching you." Her smile was so warm and generous.

"You think so?" I asked. "Yes, you will see me up there. Vance and me."

Vance shrugged and looked at the floor. It was a little annoying. I wished he wouldn't be so flip about everything. But seeing the Dance Theatre of Harlem was so exciting, nothing could dampen my mood.

I didn't want the performance to end. When it did, and Vance was driving me home, I rested against the backseat, lost in my daydreams of being on stage, hearing the applause. I replayed the show in my mind, casting myself into the principal parts. All I had to do was continue to work hard and I could do it. A year from now, I'd go to New York, take class with the company again. Arthur Mitchell would be so astounded by my progress, he'd offer me a place in his company. . . .

Vance parked in front of my house.

I got out of the car after thanking Miss Winnie one more

time. But to my surprise, Vance got out of the car, too. "I'll walk you to the door," he said.

My heart raced as we walked up my driveway. Why was he walking me to the door? He'd never done that before. Would he kiss me good night? But Miss Winnie was sitting in the car, surely he wouldn't—and what if my parents, sitting up for me I'm sure, opened the door?

Once we were standing at my doorstep, I faced him, not knowing what to do. He was standing close, but not close enough to kiss me. He just stood there, his hands in his pockets.

"Well, here I am!" I said, then wished I hadn't. It was all I could do to keep myself from wincing with embarrassment.

A hand came out of his pocket, and he sort of clapped me on the shoulder. "Hey, me and the fellas are dancing at Club Infinity Friday night. Wanna come?"

"Club Infinity?" I repeated like a fool.

"After rehearsal Friday night. What do you say?"

"Um, sure . . ." I said. "But I don't know what time I'll have to be home."

He shrugged. "I'll get you home on time, whenever that is."

"Okay." I smiled now, but he didn't take the puny hint I gave him.

"All right. See you Friday in rehearsal, then." With that, he turned his back to me and crossed the front lawn to his car.

I waved to Miss Winnie, then I used my key to open the door.

"Stephanie!" Mom and Dad were both sitting in the den as I came in, waiting up for me, obviously. "How was the performance?" Mom asked me.

"It was great. The company, they were great. . . ." I shifted back and forth on my heels, hoping I could avoid the third degree. I didn't know what to think of Vance at all. I was exhilarated from tonight and excited about the prospect of going out with him Friday night.

"What about the dance class?" Dad asked.

"Great. Arthur Mitchell, he's the company's founder, he told Vance and me we should come take class with the company again in a year," I said. "And it's all because of Miss Winnie. She's really helping me to become a better dancer."

"This Miss Winnie isn't planning on having you miss school to take more dance classes, is she?" Dad asked.

"Well, the Dance Theatre of Harlem doesn't come to town every day!"

Dad looked me in the eye. "No need for that tone of voice, Stephanie. I was talking about the next ballet company that comes to town. I want to make it clear that—"

"This was a one-time thing, I know," I said, stewing. Why couldn't they just let me enjoy the night? Why did they have to be so disapproving all the time?

I backed out of the den. "I'm really tired. It's been a long day." I went downstairs and was quickly in bed, dreaming about the Dance Theatre of Harlem as I drifted off to sleep.

sixteen

The Prologue of *The Sleeping Beauty* was starting to come together. What at first seemed like a chaotic mass of bodies was starting to look like an actual ballet. We began Friday's rehearsal with the Fairies' entrance, in which each of the Fairies is lifted high in the air by her Cavalier and carried on stage. Chris had just lifted me and was ready to carry me to center stage when Madame Caroline stopped the tape. "Camilla and Marty are out of place," she said. She marched over to the line of Fairies and their Cavaliers, took Marty and Camilla each by the hand, and led them to their proper place in line. Marty, who had just figured out how to lift Camilla like a dancer instead of a dumbbell, was bright red from embarrassment. I forget, sometimes, that dancers are used to being told what they're doing wrong all the time. But for someone new to ballet, corrections could sound like ridicule. Camilla winked at Marty. His blush deepened.

Once everyone was in place, I was lifted into the air and carried center stage, where I then commanded everyone to dance. The Prologue is when I do most of my dancing. The Princess Aurora's just a doll in the cradle at this point, so I'm the focus of attention. My solo variation's fun to dance. It's full of *pirouettes* and flying leaps. And there's an extended section where all of the Fairies and their partners dance pas de deux together, with lots of slow promenades, overhead lifts, and supported *pirouettes.* My last major section is a pantomime where I explain that the Princess Aurora will not prick her finger on an old woman's spindle and die, but will sleep for a hundred years and be awakened by the Prince. I saw Vance out of the corner of my eye as I did the pantomime. He looked bored.

Near the end of the rehearsal, Anna wandered into the studio and sat in a corner. She was dressed in a gray leotard and pointe shoes, her hair in a scraggly ponytail. I figured she had a rehearsal after us. Having her in the studio made me work harder, lift my leg higher in *arabesque.* I'm not really sure why. Since the Pacific Northwest audition, we hadn't really talked. She still showed up for class five minutes beforehand and left directly afterward.

At the end of rehearsal, when I was going over a partnering sequence with Chris, Vance interrupted me. "It'll be a little while," he said, wiping sweat from his forehead. "I'm supposed to go over something with Anna."

"Sure," I said.

Chris raised his eyebrows as Vance walked away. "You've got plans?"

"He's dancing at a nightclub tonight, and he asked me to come." Eager to change the subject, I said, "Is it true your wife's having a baby?"

Chris looked proud. "She's four months along."

"Wow." I remembered what Camilla had said about having a baby on a tiny corps de ballet salary. "Congratulations."

He clapped me on the shoulder and went to the men's dressing room.

I didn't want to make the same mistake I had made when I went to that party with Gillian, so this time I wore jeans and a tank top. In my dance bag, I had brought a blow dryer and a curling iron so I could fix my hair in the bathroom. I even put on a little bit of makeup.

Once I looked as good as I was going to, I went to the studio to see how Vance and Anna's rehearsal was going. I couldn't help but feel a stab of envy as I watched them rehearsing the final wedding scene pas de deux. Bridget had said Anna and Vance would look funny together on stage, but watching them now, I disagreed. His darkness seemed to complement her paleness. Madame Caroline took Anna aside to give her some corrections and waved Vance away, apparently dismissing him for the night. Madame Caroline watched Anna perform her solo variation, stopping her every few moments to fix an arm or a turn of the head. It was like Anna was the only living creature in the universe, that's how intent Madame Caroline's gaze was. *At least you have Miss Winnie,* I told myself.

Vance crossed the lobby on the way to the men's dressing room. "I'll be out soon," he said, and sure enough, he appeared five minutes later, smelling soapy fresh. He wore baggy white pants with a black button-down shirt. He looked as if he was ready to go to a dance club a lot more than I did in my jeans. I wondered if I had dressed wrong again. "C'mon," he said. I followed him up the stairs and outside to Miss Winnie's car.

"How did rehearsal with Anna go?" I asked as he drove out of the parking lot.

His shoulders went up and down. "I'll be glad when all this is over."

"You mean *Sleeping Beauty*?"

"I mean all this." His face was expressionless. "We'll probably win tonight."

"You and your friends? When did you start dancing with them, anyway?"

"You know, you watch videos, you copy the moves."

"But your friends don't know you do ballet."

Vance shook his head slightly. I suddenly remembered how Gillian had said her new guy friend, Frankie, knew Vance. She had told them how she'd seen Vance at the ballet studio.

"Do you know a guy named Frankie? At your school?" I asked him.

"Frankie? Frankie who?"

"I don't know his last name. This girl I go to school with knows him and he says he knows you."

"I think I know who you're talking about." His face showed nothing, so I had no idea what Vance thought of this guy. He drove to a part of town I'd never been to before. The neighborhood looked a lot like mine, sort of working-class and ordinary.

"Where are we?"

"Montbello." He parked the car in what looked like any lower-middle-class-type strip mall. Even in the dark, I could tell the place had seen better days. The only brightness came from a large neon sign in one corner blazing INFINITY in big blue letters.

I grew nervous. "Do you . . . drink?"

"No. This is a teen club. The only alcohol here is what folks sneak in."

It was too bad we were here already. To tell the truth, I didn't care about being at the club. I just wanted to talk to Vance. My nerves frayed as we approached the club and I saw the line snaking out the door. The kids were mostly black and Mexican, wearing brightly colored versions of either really saggy or really tight clothes. A few people wore regular jeans like me. I'd never been to a club before. At the few school dances I attended last year, I'd go out on the dance floor with girls who used to take ballet with me but have since graduated. And I've watched BET *Video Soul* on TV; the dancing in music videos wasn't anything I couldn't do. Still, I couldn't help but feel self-conscious.

Vance slapped hands with some people in line, but to my surprise he led me past the line directly to the door. A tall, muscular man in a tight black T-shirt waved us in.

"Why the special treatment?" I had to shout; the music was blaring.

"I come here a lot," he shouted back. He took my hand now, mainly not to lose me as we wove our way through the crowd. The sudden warmth of the packed room after the coolness of the night was like stepping into a sauna. I could hardly see anything from the dark blue light and swirls of smoke. Spotlights flashed in short bursts over the dance floor, where bodies writhed in silhouette. Vance led me to a able near the back of the club. "Want something to drink?"

"A Coke."

He left me sitting there as he went to the bar. I looked around as my eyes adjusted to the darkness. Along the back wall, I could see boys and girls pressed against one another.

Vance returned with two Cokes and sat in a chair next to me.

"So when does the dance contest start?" I shouted over the noise.

"A little later. This place gets really packed," Vance said. "You like it?"

I shrugged. I felt more overwhelmed than anything else. But he just nodded with a little smile, like I had given him an answer. I watched him as his eyes scanned the crowded room. He looked relaxed to me, but he didn't really look like he belonged here with all the clumps of girls in tiny microdresses and the guys weaving in and out with their come-ons and studied moves.

Across the room, I saw a familiar hank of curly black hair. When the girl turned in profile to smile teasingly at the boy next to her, I realized it was Gillian.

She looked great. She wore a silver minidress with matching silver high heels. The shoes were a color that told me they matched only the outfit she was wearing and absolutely nothing else, and they were probably expensive. When she turned around, her eyes widened. She whispered something to the boy next to her, and they headed toward our table.

The boy she was with was certainly handsome and expensively dressed. As handsome as he was, though, I thought there was a slick look to him. He didn't look like someone I would instinctively trust. I figured he was Frankie. Another guy was coming toward us with Gillian and Frankie, and I figured he was the one Gillian had wanted me to meet. He wore his hair in neat cornrows and had the same slick look as Frankie.

Vance sat up a little as he saw them approaching us. His eyes narrowed slightly and I knew these were no friends of his.

"I go to school with that girl," I said to Vance. "Her name's Gillian."

"Steph! Hey, girl!" Gillian teetered on her high heels, then threw her arms around my neck. I stiffened at her touch. Her hair and skin stank of smoke, just like Camilla's had. "This's Frankie and Clay." She took Frankie's hand to steady herself. She'd been drinking. A lot, by the look of it.

"What's up?" Frankie looked at Vance in a sort of mocking way. Vance, still slumped in his chair, returned a "what's up" that sounded equally cold to me. Clay and Frankie joined us at our table. Gillian sat on Frankie's lap.

"I didn't think you'd be here," Gillian slurred. "You gotta do ballet all the time—I told you, Frankie, Steph's a ballerina." Gillian was making a fool of herself, I thought, but her friends didn't seem to mind. The haze of lights and smoke in the club made my eyes sting.

"This is the guy who dances." Gillian pointed at Vance. "He dances ballerina."

Clay laughed now. "You mean you go swishing around on your toes, wearing tights and all?" He made some loose-wristed flutterings with his hands.

Gillian giggled, but Vance said nothing.

"Come on, show us some twinkle-toes, man!" Now Frankie got in on the act. "You're dancing tonight, right? Gonna get up there and do some ballet?"

They were all laughing: Gillian, Clay, and Frankie. I sat

there tight-lipped, burning with anger. But Vance looked vacant, almost as if he didn't hear them.

"C'mon," he said to me, standing up.

"Gonna go out on the dance floor now and show us some ballet?" Clay asked.

I gave him the dirtiest look I could muster as I took Vance's hand and we walked away from the table. Vance led me onto the dance floor, and we disappeared into the mass of writhing bodies. He held me close as we danced together, mainly because there wasn't much room. The music was deafening and sweaty bodies bumped into me. "Just forget about them," I shouted into Vance's ear, the only way we could talk.

He didn't answer. His arm went around my waist and we swayed together. My heart pulsed, with anger as much as with the excitement of dancing so close to Vance. I thought of Gillian, throwing her arms around me one minute, then laughing at Vance and me the next. I didn't think I wanted to have anything to do with her ever again.

Two guys dressed like Vance in white pants and black shirts approached us. Vance pulled away from me and slapped hands with them. "This is Corey and James," Vance shouted. Both of the guys smiled and nodded at me. It was hard to see their faces with the strobe light pulsing and flickering. They said something to Vance that I couldn't hear, and then Vance took my hand and led me away from the dance floor. We followed Vance's friends to a narrow hallway. My face and neck felt sticky with sweat, from the heat of so many bodies pressed together more than anything.

The music stopped, and the dance floor was quickly cleared. An emcee with a microphone ran onto the dance floor, receiving cheers from the audience. He shouted something about the dance contest. Apparently, the group with the loudest applause from the audience would get first prize. I didn't quite hear what the prize was. I looked at Vance as he stood with his friends. They looked confident and cocky, not the least bit nervous.

The first group, two girls and a guy who looked like they were improvising on stage, were quickly booed by the audience. Another group of girls in matching short-shorts and halter tops got whistles of approval from the guys in the club, but their dance consisted mostly of sexy posing. Another group of boys got everyone in the club clapping and dancing along with them. Then Vance and his friends went on. A few wolf whistles came from the direction of Gillian and her friends, but everyone else applauded, as if Vance and his group were well known.

The music started and they danced a routine with lots of big exaggerated movements, swiveling hips, and even a section where one of the boys did a back flip as Vance rolled on the floor underneath him. They danced double-time and half-time, and the audience shrieked in response. But my eyes stayed on Vance. It was as if he came alive when he danced, beads of sweat flying off his forehead, his face alternately teasing, confident, seductive. Vance knew how to play the crowd—and it seemed as if he had the entire crowd in the palm of his hand.

The contest ended, and Vance and his friends were the undisputed winners. Vance slapped high-fives with his friends as they received a check from the emcee. Watching from my place against the wall, I saw some of the girls from the short-shorts routine siddle Vance, put their arms around him, smile up in his face. I gasped, the air like a razor in my throat. What could I do? Go and intercede? What if Vance gave me the brush-off?

But he was looking around the club, and I sighed with relief. I stepped forward and Vance took my hand again. His forehead glistened, and his shirt stuck to his chest.

"You looked great out there," I said.

He shrugged a little. "You gotta get home soon, right?"

I nodded. It was getting late. He led me out of the club, and I breathed deeply as I stepped into the night, the breeze like a kiss on my face. My ears were ringing uncomfortably, and I had the beginnings of a headache. Vance wiped his face, his shoulders heaving. The stench of smoke surrounded both of us. We got into Miss Winnie's car, and he turned on the ignition.

"You're a really good dancer," I said.

"Yeah." He said this like a matter of fact, not arrogance.

"I could tell how much you like dancing like that, dancing for the crowd."

"It's pretty cool." The car hummed as he drove onto a darkened street.

"You like it better than ballet, don't you?" I looked out the window as I said this.

"I can't tell Miss Winnie that."

I turned to him. "Why not?"

"You know how she is. Ballet for her, it's like religion or something."

"But why do you have to choose one or the other?"

"Why do I have to do both?" He sounded bitter.

"It's hard for a guy to say he does ballet," I said. "I know it sucked listening to those guys rag on you."

"It doesn't matter."

"But it does! People make fun of guys who say they like ballet. So I guess you'd have to do something like club dancing so people won't think—" I stopped because he wasn't listening to me anymore. He stared straight forward, blank-faced, like he was shutting me out completely.

"Do you just not want to talk about it?" I asked.

"What's to talk about? You already have all the answers."

His tone of voice wounded me. "I was just trying to say I know what it feels like to get made fun of."

"Yeah?"

"That girl Gillian? I went to a party with her a few weeks ago. Remember how I showed up at Miss Winnie's late one night? The party was a disaster."

"How?"

"This guy was teasing me about my father being a janitor at school."

"What'd you do?"

I blushed, thinking about it. "I threw a beer in his face."

Vance laughed out loud.

"I didn't think about it, I just did it! And then afterward, I felt like such an idiot—I called Miss Winnie and asked if I could come stay at her house."

Vance didn't say anything, but I know he heard me, and I know he understood. Still, I leaned against the window, frustrated. Why was Vance so difficult to penetrate? Why wouldn't he just open up to me?

All too soon, he parked in front of my house. The light in the kitchen was on. Someone was waiting up for me.

"I guess I'll see you at rehearsal tomorrow," I said. I wondered if he was going to walk me to the door.

He gave no indication of moving. "What are we rehearsing tomorrow, anyway?"

"The vision scene, I think. Thanks for bringing me to the club."

"Yeah, I'm glad you came." He paused, then he leaned toward me and put an arm around my shoulder. My cheek pressed against his damp shirt for a moment. His neck radiated warmth. Then he released me, and I got out of the car to take the solitary walk to my doorstep.

seventeen

All of us from Madame Caroline's class were at the Colorado Ballet Academy on Wednesday. I stood in the dressing room with Anna, Camilla, Ursula, and Bridget as we got ready for the School of American Ballet summer program audition. I was less nervous this time, mainly from having gone through the Pacific Northwest audition a few weeks ago. Besides, if I could take class with the Dance Theatre of Harlem and not feel like an incompetent idiot, I could get through this audition as well.

"I can't believe you're so calm!" Bridget exclaimed as she pinned flowers to her bun.

"Relax," I said. "It'll be okay." All of us were trying to do something to stand out: silk flowers, a colorful hair ribbon, all in the hope of getting noticed amid the crowd of talented, thin dancers. I had circled my bun with gold braid, which I thought looked pretty against my black hair. It made me feel almost regal, the way Miss Winnie looked in her gold turban. We'd all heard that the judges, who were either teachers from the School of American Ballet or dancers with the New York City Ballet, would know who they wanted and who they didn't want as soon as we walked into the room. That seemed so unfair to me, the fact that we would all be judged before we had done one single dance step. But any time nervousness crept into the back of my mind, I quashed it. Miss Winnie had told me on Sunday, "Walk into that room with confidence, like you believe you're the best dancer there."

That's what I was planning to do, to seem confident without appearing stuck-up. I'd hold my head high and I'd stand up straight, but I would smile, too. But even Anna's face was deathly pale from anxiety as she put on her ballet slippers. Ursula cowered in a corner, near tears. The only reason she was here was that Madame Caroline insisted that we all come. She would even be in the audition studio, watching. Camilla looked bored, but I could tell her bored expression masked her nerves, too.

"SAB cattle call, here we come!" she said. "All you cows ready?"

Bridget giggled. "Camilla!"

Camilla hooted. "Come on, we can't take all this too seriously! I should've dyed my hair purple. Then the judges would have to notice me!"

Ursula squeezed her eyes shut, and I thought she looked ill.

I sat next to her on a bench and put an arm around her shaking shoulders. "Relax."

"I can't go through with this," she mumbled. "I can't do it."

"Of course you can!" I squeezed her shoulders. "It's just a ballet class."

Her eyes were big and fearful. "Will they make us leave if they don't like us?"

"No, they don't do that!" I said. "That's just a rumor."

Camilla laughed again. "No, it isn't. They'll take one look at my flat feet and shove me out the door!"

"Oh, shut up," I said.

To my surprise, Anna sat on the other side of Ursula. "Everyone takes the whole class. Madame Caroline said so."

Ursula smiled, looking grateful.

I took a deep breath and stood up. "Let's go!"

All twelve of us from Madame Caroline's class left the dressing room and squeezed our way through the crowded hallway to the lobby.

Miss Winnie sat in the lobby with Vance. I went right to them. Miss Winnie looked more anxious than Vance did, who sat slumped over, elbows on knees. "Take a place right near the front," she was telling Vance. "You want to make sure they see you—Stephanie!" She stood up and hugged me. "You remember what I told you?"

I nodded.

She smiled. "Show them what you can do."

"I will. Thanks." I went back to my friends from ballet class. They were all looking at me in a wistful way.

"That's so great." Bridget gave a little sigh. "Having that lady helping you, working with you."

It made such a difference, having someone believe in me. Anna had that with Madame Caroline, but what about Bridget, Camilla, Ursula, the rest?

"Oh my God, check her out!" Camilla nodded toward a large girl standing by the door. I say large because she was, well, the biggest person I've ever seen in a leotard and tights. She had to be five feet nine or ten, and I'd say close to one hundred and eighty pounds. She had dark skin and black hair slicked back in a tight bun. She looked foreign to me, Filipino maybe, or Polynesian. I wouldn't call her fat; her body looked firm in its leotard and tights, but she was definitely heavyset. She did *pliés* by herself, holding on to the wall for support.

"She has good turnout," Camilla said, shrugging.

I glanced across the lobby at Miss Winnie, who was looking at the large girl, too. I couldn't read her expression. It seemed as if everyone was stealing glances, whispering about her. My face grew warm with embarrassment for her. I knew what it was like to be stared at at an audition. Still, I couldn't help but wonder what she was doing here, too, knowing how strict and exacting the School of American Ballet was about body types. I wasn't even sure if I had the right body type.

"She must've gotten lost," I heard a girl from another studio whisper, but it was a whisper loud enough to be heard.

"Yeah, Weight Watchers is across the street!" another girl said, and laughed.

All of us in Madame Caroline's class looked at one another, frowning.

"I hope they suck," Camilla muttered.

I looked at the large girl, who continued to do *pliés,* ignoring the commotion. But she had to know that everyone was staring at her. She wore a purple leotard with shiny salmon-pink tights that I thought only accentuated her thick legs. Her face showed nothing, proudly blank with the kind of self-assurance I'd seen on the faces of so many narrow-hipped, stick-thin girls at the Pacific Northwest Ballet School audition.

The doors of the studio opened and we all rushed inside. My nose was overwhelmed with the smell of perfume, hairspray, Ben-Gay, baby powder. Two women and a man sat in the front of the studio on folding chairs. Holding Ursula's hand, I led us to spaces at the barre right in front of the judges. Anna, Camilla, and Bridget stood with us. I craned my eyes for Vance, who took a place near the back. I tried to get his attention, but I was afraid I would lose my place if I moved.

The two girls who made those bitchy comments stood at my barre. Both of them wore black leotards and white flowers pinned in their hair. They both had perfect turnout, perfect feet, and the smugness that came with the knowledge of that perfection. I hated them both.

To my surprise, the large girl motioned beside me, as if she wondered if the place was taken. I nodded and smiled, and she rested her hand on the barre. The two bitchy girls looked at each other with their lips pressed together, like they were suppressing laughter.

I felt good during barre. My technique was strong, and I executed the combinations well. All of the tedious work with Miss Winnie was really showing results. But I was nervous when barre ended and we all came to center floor. During barre, I couldn't really pay attention to the judges, where they were looking. In center floor, it would be painfully clear who they were watching and who they were ignoring.

I watched the large girl execute the *adagio.* Her leg extensions weren't great, but she danced with fluidity and control. During the *pirouette* combination she spun like a top, doing triple and quadruple *pirouettes* to the left and to the right when most everyone else was doing doubles. I realized she wasn't just a large person dancing competently. There was a lyrical quality to her that made me want to watch her dance. I had watched the two bitchy girls do triple and quadruple *pirouettes,* too, but to me they were simply executing technique, not dancing. I hadn't comprehended before today the difference between the two. Even Madame Caroline, sitting in her folding chair, was watching the large girl. But were the judges?

As for me, I thought the audition was relatively easy. I didn't make any mistakes in the combinations, and I saw a judge nod at me as I did a triple *pirouette.* Vance didn't seem to be into the audition at all. He marked steps instead of dancing full-out, with a bored, I-don't-care expression on his face. Madame Caroline crossed her arms across her chest and frowned at him. As I watched him sleepwalk his way through the *petit allegro,* I grew angry as well. Why wasn't he really trying? Was he getting smug and complacent? Did he just not care?

After the class was over, the judges kept maybe ten of us behind. My heart leaped as the instructor pointed to me, and I couldn't help but smile to see Bridget's eyes glowing as she was asked to stay, too. She squeezed my hand as we stood with Anna, the only other girl from our studio invited to remain. Vance filed out with everyone else, not even glancing my way. When the room cleared, the large girl was nowhere to be seen.

The judges didn't keep us long. They spent maybe five minutes on each of us, manipulating our feet with their hands, lifting our legs to the front and side to test our flexibility. Their faces revealed nothing at all. They just went about their business, scribbling notes on their forms.

When they let us out of the room, Bridget couldn't stop chattering. "Now we have a better chance of getting picked, don't we? Do you think they'll remember us after they go around to all those different cities?" Bridget paused, staring in the direction of the large girl. She stood in a corner, pulling a pair of jeans over those shiny pink tights. Bridget cocked her head to the side, as if she wasn't sure what to think.

"She was amazing," Bridget said finally. I noticed other girls from the audition glancing at her in astonished admiration as they whispered among themselves.

Camilla and Ursula met us in the dressing room. I could see the disappointment in both of their faces in not being asked to stay after the audition, although Camilla tried to hide her feelings behind her usual sarcasm. "So when are you folks heading out to New York City?"

"They just looked at out legs and feet," I said. "It doesn't mean anything."

Camilla shrugged. Her eyes turned to the large girl. "I guess they didn't want to look at her legs and feet."

"They should!" Ursula said stubbornly. "Instead of some stick-figure bunhead."

It seemed so unfair to me, how that girl wasn't really given a chance. She was the only dancer in the room who really moved me, made me want to watch her dance. If she could do that in an audition, I'm sure she could do that on stage. So why shouldn't a company want her?

After getting dressed, I went up to the lobby to wait for Vance and Miss Winnie. Madame Caroline stood next to Miss Winnie in the lobby, the two of them huddled together. Miss Winnie's face was creased with anger. Vance was nowhere to be seen.

Madame Caroline turned to me with her arms folded over her chest. She peered at me from under her narrow glasses. "Nice work. Your technique is getting much stronger."

I blinked, amazed. That was the nicest thing Madame Caroline had said to me in a long time—maybe ever! "Thank you." I glanced at Miss Winnie. "I've been working really hard."

Miss Winnie smiled back at me.

Madame Caroline nodded. "Keep it up," she said before walking away.

"It felt good," I said to Miss Winnie. "They looked at my legs and feet, just like Arthur Mitchell did."

"I'm so proud of you." Miss Winnie hugged me. But then her face clouded over, and the lines in her face deepened. I'd never seen her look angrier. I had always considered her to be above anger somehow, like she was so absorbed with love and warmth and beauty that anger was an emotion she had no interest in. Even when I overheard her talking to Vance that Saturday morning, Vance was the one who had sounded angry, not Miss Winnie.

"I'll have to say a few words to that nephew of mine!" she said. Madame Caroline must have given her a report on the audition.

"He didn't make many mistakes—" For some reason, I felt like I had to cover for him.

Miss Winnie seemed furious. "To have so much talent, to waste an opportunity. He has no right, I tell you! No right at all!"

"Um, Vance really did fine." My voice was edgy as I spoke. "Really, he was the best guy in there. They had to notice him."

Miss Winnie snatched her purse from a chair, still frowning. As much as I cared about her feelings, I couldn't help but wonder if she was taking it all a little too personally.

"The San Francisco Ballet School's audition is this Friday," I said. "I'll see you and Vance there, right?"

Miss Winnie smiled now, looking hopeful once more. "Of course you will. I wouldn't miss it."

Bridget appeared in the lobby, motioning that her mother had arrived to pick us up.

I backed away from Miss Winnie. "I have to go. I'll see you Friday."

"All right," she said.

eighteen

I left the building feeling exhausted. No, drained, really, is a better word. I couldn't stop thinking about Vance, why he blew the audition the way he did. I replayed the conversation from last Friday as Mrs. Alfonso drove me home. I'll be glad when all this is over, Vance had said. But I was so caught up in my weird feelings—being out on what could be called my first sort of "date"—that I didn't really consider what that meant. Yes, I saw how much he loved dancing with his friends at the club, but how could that compare to the feeling that comes from ballet? And if he really didn't want to do ballet anymore, then how could he tell Miss Winnie? He had no right to blow the audition, Miss Winnie had said, like her desire for his success had taken that "right" away from him. My forehead throbbed painfully. It was all I could do to mumble one-word responses to Mrs. Alfonso's questions about the audition.

I mumbled a thank-you to Mrs. Alfonso when she dropped me off in front of my house. My next obstacle was to sneak past my parents to my room, where I could be alone with all of my strange, disturbed feelings.

I had no such luck. Mom and Dad were both sitting at the dinner table, waiting for me. Half-eaten plates of spaghetti lay before them; I had told them not to hold up dinner for me. My stomach rumbled at the aroma of spaghetti sauce, but I was too out of sorts to eat with them at the table. Maybe I'd eat later, after they had gone to the den to watch TV.

"How'd the audition go?" Mom asked. She immediately began dumping spaghetti onto a plate for me.

"Fine. I think I'll eat a little later. I'm tired." I was about to turn around and go to my room, but Dad interrupted me.

"Why can't you join us at the table?" He sounded stern.

"Because I'm tired, okay?" I sounded snappier than I'd meant to. I was just so torn up inside over Vance and Miss Winnie.

"I've almost had enough of this." Dad threw his napkin on the table. Mom's face wore the grave look that told me she was expecting a showdown between Dad and me.

I sucked in a deep breath, then huffed it out. "Look, I've been dancing for two hours and I'm tired. All I want to do is go downstairs and rest."

Dad glared at me. "We never see you anymore. You never speak to us." His voice rose. "You come into this house and go downstairs to your room without so much as a word to either me or your mother!"

"That's because whenever we do talk, all you do is nag me about ballet!" I shot back. I dropped my dance bag to my side and glared back at my father.

His face was taut. Both of his hands were pressed against the table, as if he'd launch himself to his feet at any moment. His eyes, fatigued as they looked, blazed fire at me. But when he spoke, his voice was even. "I think it's time you cut back on ballet."

I felt a chuckle catch in my throat, and I looked up at the ceiling a moment. I had to repeat his words in my head to make sure I'd heard him right. "I don't believe I'm hearing this."

Dad went on as if he hadn't heard me. "The long hours, the fatigue, the time away from your family. It's all too much!"

"No." I shook my head, my neck stiff with tension. "No way."

Dad's eyes widened, almost as if he couldn't believe I was saying no to his face. "You're still our daughter, Stephanie. You'll do as you're told."

"No, I won't." I shot back. "Not if it means giving up ballet. Never!"

"Your father never said anything about giving up." Mom was trying to sound soothing, but her voice was strained. "He just thinks you should cut back a little—"

But I couldn't listen to anything she or Dad had to say. "No way! I have to dance and you can't stop me. I won't let you stop me! Because if you try, then I'll run away and live with Miss Winnie. I will!"

"You're spending entirely too much time with that woman—" Dad began, but I cut him off with a loud *no* that made my chest hurt. That was the wrong thing to say to me. No way could I listen to Dad say anything about Miss Winnie!

"Miss Winnie believes in me!" I shouted. "She believes in me more than you ever will! I wish I lived with her instead of with you!"

Mom and Dad were staring at me, openmouthed, but I couldn't stop. The words poured out of my mouth like poison.

"Miss Winnie's the best thing that ever happened to me! And you know what? She tried to have a ballet career when no one wanted her, no one thought she could do it. But she had one anyway! She went to Europe, and she chased her dream. And that's what I'm going to do, too. I'm not going to push paper around an office or clean up cafeterias; I'm gonna be somebody important. And you can't stop me!"

My breathing was heavy and raspy, but it wasn't until I saw my mother's eyes glaze over that I realized I was sobbing. I stood there, watching Mom's shell-shocked face. And Dad—he blinked several times, then his head drooped forward just a few inches, so I could no longer see his face. I'd hurt him. But worse than that, I had disappointed him.

Any words I could have said choked up in my throat, blocked by my sobbing. I couldn't look at either Mom or Dad anymore. And I didn't want to look at myself at all. I wanted to be in Miss Winnie's studio, leaping around the room until the physical fatigue dulled the pain in my chest. I wanted to dance until my mind went numb, until I was ready to collapse with that wonderful sort of exhaustion that consumes all feelings.

Another onslaught of fresh sobs racked my chest, and I turned and ran out of the kitchen and out of the house. I felt horrible, like I was a horrible human being.

My sobs lessened to uncontrollable shaking as I walked briskly up the street, with no idea where I was going. I had nothing on me: no purse and no money. I wore a ratty cardigan over my leotard, which was still damp with sweat from the audition. I couldn't go back into the house, face my parents. But where could I go? What could I do? Miss Winnie immediately came to mind, but the person I truly wanted to talk to was Vance.

I hadn't seen him leave the audition. I didn't know if he was with Miss Winnie, with his friends, or with someone else I didn't know. But once the thought came to me, I was overcome with the desire to find him, speak to him. It was as if he was the only person who could understand what was going on with me.

I came to a gas station about a block from my house. My arms were clasped tight over my chest, but they did little to shield me from the chilly night air. I went to a phone book and called Miss Winnie collect. I hoped she wouldn't mind.

The phone rang four times before I heard the click of a connection on the other end.

The voice that said "hello" was listless and gruff, but I recognized it right away. "Vance!"

"Stephanie?" My heart pounded at the sound of his voice saying my name.

"I have to speak to you. Right now. Can you come pick me up?"

"Where are you?" Vance spoke in a near-mumble, as if he didn't want to be heard. I thought I heard a door slam on the other end.

I told him where I was and sat on the curb, pressing my arms into my rib cage, trying to still my shivering. I was afraid my parents would come looking for me. Maybe they'd even call for me, like they did when I was little and playing at a nearby neighbor's house. For a moment I saw myself as a little girl, trotting home at the sound of Dad's voice bellowing "Stephanie!" My eyes blurred over. I hoped Vance would come quickly.

My teeth chattered, and I shut my eyes against the wind.

"Vance, get here," I said under my breath. The street was quiet; no cars passed in front of me. The road blurred over again, and I blinked rapidly to stave off tears. I didn't want to be crying when Vance came. But the tears wouldn't stop once they started. Maybe all of this was his fault. Why did he blow the audition today and upset Miss Winnie like that? Maybe Miss Winnie was right; he had no right to do that!

But then the familiar burgundy sedan turned the corner, slowing to a stop in front of me. I wiped my face quickly, then hurried into the front seat of the car.

nineteen

We didn't talk. Not at first. Vance took his hands off the steering wheel and slumped down in the front seat. He still wore his gray sweats, with a battered jean jacket over his white tank top. His silence seemed impossible to penetrate, and that made me angrier. How could he just put a concrete wall around his emotions when mine were so raw and exposed?

I swiped a hand over my face, brushing away stray tears that lingered on my cheeks. My eyes were probably red-rimmed and swollen, but I was beyond caring what I looked like.

Vance sat up. His face was carefully blank, like he had arranged it that way to hide what he was thinking. "So where do you want to go?" His voice was as flat as his expression.

"I don't know. Away from here." My voice was equally flat.

Vance headed out of my neighborhood and onto the highway. The radio was off, and he drove in silence.

"How's Miss Winnie?"

I heard Vance sigh. His face, in profile as he watched the road, remained blank.

"She's mad because you blew off the audition." I faced him, my seat belt pressing uncomfortably against my stomach. "I watched you. You weren't even trying. Why?"

"Why is it your business?"

"If you upset Miss Winnie, it is my business!"

"Why? She's not your family. She's not your aunt."

"She's my friend. She's done a lot for me!"

Vance wrinkled his nose, as if my loud voice irritated him.

I tried to level my voice. "You should've skipped the audition if you didn't want to go."

"I didn't have a choice!" Vance raised his voice now, and when he glanced at me, his eyes were narrowed with anger. "Whatever Miss Winnie says goes."

"I don't believe you."

"Yeah? You try living with someone who talks ballet all day long, who makes you practice ballet every damn day. 'You have to dance.' " Vance did a cruel mimic of Miss Winnie. " 'If you don't dance you're good for crap!' "

"I don't believe you." Miss Winnie made us work hard, but she was never, ever cruel. "I don't believe she said that!"

"She might as well say it," Vance said. "But me and the fellas, we're thinking about heading out west or something, trying to get into music videos."

"That sounds crazy—"

"But it's what I want. Not ballet!"

So he'd said it. The silence in the car was unbearable. I didn't know what to say at all. We were on the interstate now, heading west toward the mountains. We were gaining speed, whizzing by cars as the road inclined upward. "Slow down," I said.

Without a word, Vance switched lanes and slowed down.

"You don't want to do ballet?" It hurt me to say that.

Vance sighed again, a long, drawn-out sigh that sounded as if it was full of the emotion he wouldn't show on his face. "I don't know. At first, when I was a little kid, it was like, man—I could get out of my house, away from all the racket there, and hang out with Miss Winnie—"

"Why would you want to get away from your house?" I cut in.

"My mom's only fifteen years older than me, if that tells you anything."

"It tells me you have a young mother."

"My grandma, who's Miss Winnie's sister, she took care of me a lot when I was little. But Ma, she kept trying to say she wanted to take care of me. I think she was trying to get back at Grandma more than anything else. Grandma thinks she's irresponsible. So I'd go to Ma's place, and she'd have all these guys over, drinking and stuff. But then whenever I was at Grandma's, she'd just talk about Ma, what a bad person she thought Ma was.

"The only place where folks weren't insane was Miss Winnie's house, so I'd go there. I guess she figured she could teach me ballet. She made a game out of it, called it exercise. She said if I practiced with her for an hour, then I could go out for ice cream, or go to the movies. And then she had me practicing more, almost every day. I just went along with it. As long as I could get away from Ma and Grandma, I didn't care if she made me stand on my head."

Vance shrugged. "I don't know, it was all right. I didn't

have anything else to do, really. School was a drag. I've never been all that good at it. But a couple years ago, me and a couple of guys, we started club dancing, you know? Winning contests and stuff. I liked doing that. I didn't have to be all perfect like I do in ballet."

"You don't have to be perfect—"

"What are you talking about, of course you have to be perfect! If it ain't perfect, it ain't right!" Vance sounded annoyed with me. "And I get sick of it, you know, feeling like I have to be perfect. It's just not gonna happen."

"But ballet's not about being perfect! It's about reaching for something, setting new goals for yourself all the time. That's what Miss Winnie taught me."

"Yeah, so long as the goals you set are the same as the goals she sets." Vance pulled off the interstate onto a mountain overlook. He stopped the car abruptly, making me lurch forward and brace myself against the dashboard. "You know what I said to her when we got home tonight?"

I wasn't sure I wanted to know. I wanted to rewind my life and start this day all over again, do something different to change the course of events.

"She kept going on about how disappointed she was in me for screwing up at the audition, how I was being ungrateful and all that. She said, 'Why can't you work hard like Stephanie? Why don't you appreciate everything I do for you like Stephanie?' "

I sucked in my breath. He sounded so bitter as he mimicked Miss Winnie.

"And I told her she was full of it." Vance's voice was low and deadly with its resentment. "I told her she's just trying to make another Miss Winnie out of you."

I bit my lip and clasped my trembling hands together.

Vance unbuckled his seat belt and turned around to face me. "Remember the night you came over to Miss Winnie's late? I came in from a dance contest and there you were, jumping around the studio, wearing Miss Winnie's dress. And then there comes Miss Winnie, and she starts working with you at the barre. Part of me was mad at Miss Winnie for doing that."

"Doing what?" My voice was a whisper now.

"She wasn't looking at you that night, she was looking at herself! You know what I think? I think she's never gotten over the fact that she didn't make it as a ballerina. So she's trying to live her life all over again through you."

I couldn't speak at all. I looked out the window, arcing my neck upward as if I were trying to see the stars when, in fact, I was just trying to keep the tears from spilling down my face.

"The next day I told her, 'Don't do that again. Don't ever give her one of your old dresses again.' "

I remembered coming downstairs the next morning, hearing them arguing. So that's what he had been talking about.

"She wouldn't listen to me. I don't even know why she still has her old dance dresses anyway. It's pathetic."

Tears streaked my face. I kept my head toward the window, but I didn't wipe them away. Vance was silent for a moment. I could see his faint reflection in the window. He had turned to face forward, propping his elbow against the door and his face in his hand.

"I don't know," he said finally. "Maybe you think it's okay for Miss Winnie to live her life through you, but I can't do it. It's like I can't breathe anymore. So I told her I've had it. I told her I quit."

"You quit!" I spun around to face him, forgetting, for a moment, my tearstained face. "How can you quit?"

Vance shrugged. He looked resigned, as if he'd said all he wanted to say.

"Well, what—what did she say?"

Vance placed both of his hands on the steering wheel, and I saw something break down in his face. He wasn't crying, but his face seemed heavy with all of its sadness, anger, resentment, and frustration. "She just kept saying, 'How could you do it? How could you do it?' " He sat back in his seat and looked at me. His eyes were red-rimmed, but no tears fell.

"Shoot—" He sniffled again. "The only reason I didn't quit before was because of you." But then he turned away, and I couldn't see his face anymore.

My breath was caught in my throat for a few moments. I opened my mouth as if to say something, but then closed it when nothing came out.

Vance stared out the car window.

I didn't know what to do at all. He cared about me, and this was his way of telling me. I could see that. But what could I say to him in response? It wasn't like the romance novels I read, where the heroine is overcome with joy when the guy she likes tells her he likes her back.

"It's funny you say that." My voice was shaky as I spoke. "I guess I've been wanting you to say something like . . ." My voice trailed off. He nodded a little, which told me he heard me and he understood. I let my left hand drift over to his right, and I felt his fingertips brush over mine. He wasn't holding my hand, not really, but it felt good to be touched, to feel some connection to him.

"Part of me was mad to see you wearing her dress," Vance said, almost as if he'd been talking all this time. "But then, seeing you dancing like that, and then, when Miss Winnie's pas de deux started coming together . . ." He didn't finish his thought. But he didn't have to.

"But why do you have to quit?" I cleared my throat when my voice cracked. "Why do you have to choose between ballet and something else?"

Vance didn't answer that. He just shook his head, as if it was too hard to talk about it.

"What about *Sleeping Beauty*? The show's coming up soon."

When Vance still wouldn't answer, I turned to face him.

"You made a commitment. You can't just back out! *Sleeping Beauty*, it's not about Miss Winnie, it's about you!"

"I just don't think I can do it anymore—"

"Yes, you can, you have to! Can't you just do it for me?" As soon as it was out of my mouth, I wanted to take it back. I was horrified I'd said that. What did Vance owe me, anyway? "This is all so weird," I said. "Here you are, upset at Miss Winnie for making you practice ballet so much when my parents want me to stop."

"Really?"

"That's why I called you. I had a fight with my parents. They want me to stop spending so much time with Miss Winnie, stop dancing so much."

"What'd you say?"

The tears started again. My face must've been a swollen mess. "I said I wished I lived with Miss Winnie instead of with them. I said I wanted to be someone important and not be a nobody like them."

Vance whistled and shook his head.

"I wanted to take it back, but you can't take back something after you've said it. And there they were, looking at me. They were so hurt and I'm the one who hurt them—" I was sobbing uncontrollably now. I buried my face in my hands, and I felt Vance's warm hand on my back. I turned around and suddenly he had his arms around me and I cried into his shoulder. I felt like I was being torn apart inside. I just couldn't stop crying. I cried for my parents, for hurting them the way I had. I was also crying for Miss Winnie. All of her hopes of turning me into a dancer, maybe even to make me into another version of her, it didn't make me angry the way it did Vance. It made me sad for her, sad for all of her disappointment and her feelings of failure. I was crying for Vance, too, who couldn't bring himself to show his emotions to me. But most of all I was crying for myself, my inability to deal with any of it, any of my own fears, longings, and inadequacies.

Vance just held me, stroking my back as I cried. He didn't say anything, even as my tears soaked through his shirt. My eyes were blinded by my tears and my sobs echoed in my ears. But Vance held me until my sobs diminished. I wished I had a Kleenex to wipe my runny nose. I kept swiping my hand under my nose and sniffling.

"Sorry," I muttered, but Vance shook his head, like it didn't matter.

"I should take you home," he said.

I hiccuped and sat back in my seat. I didn't want to go home, but where else could I go? And where could we really go together? "Where are you gonna stay tonight?"

Vance started the ignition. "Corey's, probably. You met him Friday night."

"But you still have Miss Winnie's car."

"I know." He headed down the gentle incline, toward Denver. I hadn't realized how far we had driven. All of the city lights glittered before us, red and green and yellow and blue. It suddenly struck me that each one of those colorful dots represented a home, and in each home resided all kinds of hopes, dreams, and ambitions. I had always looked down on the people of my neighborhood as ordinary, but what did I know about any of them?

Before I knew it, Vance had pulled up in front of my house. I sat there for a moment without reaching for the door handle, partially because I dreaded going inside to face my parents and partially because I felt like I had to say one last thing to Vance.

A scary thought occurred to me. If Vance stopped taking ballet, then how would I see him? The only way I had ever reached him was through Miss Winnie. If he wasn't going to live at her house, then what?

"Please don't quit *Sleeping Beauty*," I said. "It's just a few weeks until the show." I turned to face him, imploring him with my eyes as much as I could.

Vance looked uncomfortable for a moment. But then his eyes settled on me and he gave me a small half-smile. "All right then," he said. "I'll do it for you."

He leaned close to me then, and his lips brushed against mine. I barely felt it, with my chin still shaking so much. But then he kissed me again, more firmly this time. Right when I started to get that melty feeling I got when I danced with him, he was pulling away from me.

"You'd better go," he said.

"Yeah." I felt like I should say something else, but my mind felt empty, the kind of emptiness that comes when your brain, overloaded with feelings and emotions, simply shuts off. "I'll see you at rehearsal tomorrow?"

He paused, then nodded. "Yeah."

I waited a moment, to see if he would kiss me again, but he didn't. So I got out of the car and trudged up the yard to my house.

I've read that first kisses were sweet, electrifying, or passionate, but mine was none of these. There was a sadness to my kiss with Vance, an attempt at connection when we were both feeling so alienated and alone. But I was too tired to replay it in my mind, and too filled with dread over what I might find inside my house.

I knocked on the front door and waited. Almost immediately, I heard heavy footsteps approaching the door.

The door opened, and Dad stood in front of me. He looked stern and he looked somber, but more than anything, he looked as tired as I felt.

I braced myself for an onslaught. But strangely, Dad said nothing to me. I scooted by him and went downstairs to my room, shutting my door behind me.

twenty

I slept fitfully, tossing and turning all night long. By the time my alarm went off, I felt tired and sluggish. I wanted to turn over in bed and, if I couldn't sleep, at least lie there with the covers pulled over my head. I heard Mom and Dad walking around in the kitchen, sitting down for breakfast. I couldn't avoid them. Maybe I could get away with not talking to Dad last night, but I had to ride to school with him this morning.

Mom was sitting at the kitchen table, drinking orange juice. She said, "Hi, Stephanie" in a stiff, formal way, but she didn't look at me. I hesitated before joining her at the table. I hadn't really thought about it before, but it must be hard on Mom whenever I fight with Dad about ballet. It seems like she's always in the middle, agreeing with Dad but at least trying to see my point of view. We sat at the table in silence, eating our cereal.

Dad didn't even say hello to me. He sat at the table with his eyes on the newspaper. It looked as if he had on a new work shirt, or at least his powder blue shirt was crisply pressed.

After a few minutes of uncomfortable silence, Dad looked at his watch and said, "Time to go." I mumbled a good-bye to Mom and followed Dad out to the car.

I stared out the window on the ride to school. Dad had the radio tuned to National Public Radio, which eliminated the need for talking. Not until we drove through the wrought-iron entry of Lakeview Country Day and Dad was parking the car in the staff lot did he speak to me.

"Have a good day," he said, and walked off in the direction of his office.

I had no real desire to go into that building, face all my classmates who probably didn't know, or care, I existed anyway, other than knowing me as the janitor's daughter. I scribbled distractedly on my folders during my first two class periods. I couldn't stop thinking about Vance, how he had said school was such a drag for him. School was a drag for me, too, but that was because of the environment, not because of the academics. Yes, I had to keep above a 3.5 in order to stay in ballet, parents' orders, but that wasn't too difficult. That got me thinking, what would, or could, I do if I didn't become a dancer? I never really let myself consider any other possibility, even though I could be prevented from having a ballet career for any number of reasons. What if I had a serious, career-ending injury? Or what if I just couldn't find a place anywhere in a company? Would I then teach ballet, or try to live my life through someone else the way Miss Winnie had? It was a frightening thought. And a dance career didn't last forever; even if I did make it, I'd be lucky to dance until I was forty. So what would I do then? And who would I be? I had no answers at all; each question seemed to spawn more questions.

After second period, I picked my way through the crowded hallway. I dawdled at my locker as the crowd thinned out. I just couldn't seem to make myself move quickly. The third-period bell rang, and I was still standing at my locker. I pushed the door shut and meandered to the bathroom. Maybe I'd spend all of study hall just wandering around. It wasn't like I could concentrate on any schoolwork, anyway.

I heard a horrible retching sound coming from one of the toilets, and I almost scurried out of there. The bathroom stank of cigarette smoke and the nasty-sweet smell of illness. The retching was loud and tortured-sounding enough to make me feel queasy, too. Then I saw a familiar gold designer handbag lying on the floor.

I knocked on the toilet-stall door. "Gillian?" I'd seen only Gillian carry a purse like that. She had a different purse, if not for every outfit, at least for every color scheme in her wardrobe.

"Go away!" The voice was unmistakably Gillian's. We hadn't spoken at all since last Friday night at the club.

I knocked on the door again. "Gillian? Are you okay?"

"Leave me alone!" The words were squeezed out before an onslaught of heavy sobbing.

As much as I disliked Gillian, there was no way I could walk out of the bathroom now. "It's Stephanie. Do you need me to get the nurse?"

"No!" The retching had stopped, replaced by injured breathing. She moaned like she was in great pain, then began to cough.

"You don't want me to get the nurse? Your parents could come take you home—"

"No! You can't—" The sound of the toilet flushing drowned out her coughing.

I stood there, shifting on my feet. "What do you want me to do?"

Silence on the other end. I couldn't even hear her breathing or sobbing anymore. I got down on my hands and knees and peered under the toilet-stall door. Gillian's knees were drawn up to her chest. Her face was turned away from me as she rested her head against the metal wall, her curly hair in wild disarray. I crawled underneath the door and sat next to her.

"Gillian?"

When she turned around, it was all I could do not to gasp. She looked horrible, and I don't mean just the red puffy eyes and the face streaked with makeup. Her skin was chalky and her lips blue. She was shaking. The rank smell of alcohol was coming off of her, but she appeared sick more than drunk. She stared at the floor without speaking.

"Are you okay?" As soon as the words were out of my mouth, I knew it was a dumb thing to say. She was obviously far from okay.

Her breathing was shallow and forced. "Just leave me alone," she whispered.

"I can't leave. Not now."

She placed both hands over her face.

"Have you been drinking?"

She chuckled from behind her hands. "I'm not drunk! I can drink way more than I drank today."

I didn't tell her I didn't think that was much for her to be proud of.

"You take me to the nurse, and I'll just get thrown out of school." It seemed like she was trying to put on her usual bored, too-cool-for-this expression, but it wouldn't stay on her face.

"What happened this morning?"

"What do you care, anyway?"

"I could have just turned around and left when I heard you in here. I didn't have to come see if you were okay."

Gillian looked as if she was considering this, then she lowered her head.

"Do you want me to get Lisa or Kelly?"

Gillian shut her eyes, her lips trembling. She shook her head.

"What happened this morning?"

She shrugged, and her usual bored expression returned. "I went into my mom's medicine cabinet and took a bunch of different pills. And then I went to the liquor cabinet and poured myself a glass of vodka. It was like my head was floating a foot above my neck. I don't even know how I drove without getting in a wreck." She wiped a hand under her nose. "I got here just before study hall and as I was going to my locker, I just started feeling really sick."

She started laughing now. "I remember thinking, I could fall down the staircase and everyone would make a big deal of it, me dying at school. I could put a curse on the place—" But her laughter soon turned to sobs, deep, raspy sobs that shook her whole body. She fell against me, her hair fanning over my face.

I sat there, frozen with fear. This was too much for me; I couldn't handle this alone. What if some of those pills were still in her body? She probably needed to go to the hospital.

"Come on, we're getting up." I spoke as soothingly as I could, then I stood up slowly, pulling her to her feet. She didn't resist, but it was hard to move her because she was leaning against me, like she couldn't stand up without me. Maybe she couldn't. Trying to carry her weight and mine, I staggered out of the bathroom. Thankfully, the hallway was empty. I don't know what I could have said to explain things to a passerby.

I guided her down the staircase, as slowly and carefully as I could. She didn't want to go to the nurse, and there was only one other place I could think of to take her. I took a deep breath as I pulled her down another set of stairs to the basement. At the end of the hall was a door with a plaque reading, "Dennis Haynes, Head Custodian." I remembered Dad's distant silence in the car this morning. Maybe Dad would be furious with me for bringing Gillian here, but I had to put my tensions with Dad aside. Gillian really needed help, and I had nowhere else to turn.

"Come on," I said to her. She didn't want to move her feet at all. Her head slumped against my shoulder, her hair prickly on my face. Cigarettes, alcohol, and perfume seemed to ooze out of her pores.

I knew Dad would be there. He kept a very regular schedule. During third period he did paperwork, ordering various things the school needed, organizing supplies in his office. After third period he went around emptying teachers' classroom wastebaskets. I could hear Dad's tape recorder behind the door, soft classical music. I almost stopped when I heard a familiar solo violin playing a slow, haunting melody. It was Tchaikovsky, *The Sleeping Beauty.* The movement was from the vision scene, my pas de trois with Anna and Vance. Tears sprang to my eyes. Of course Dad had no idea I'd be dancing to that particular piece of music; he'd never seen me rehearse. But he knew it was music from the ballet.

Gillian moaned, like she was nauseated or in pain. I knocked on the door. "Dad?"

The door opened immediately. Dad's eyes widened when he saw me holding Gillian, and he ushered us inside. I eased Gillian into the chair across from Dad's desk, and she immediately slumped forward, laying her head on his desk.

"I found her in the bathroom upstairs." I spoke in a low voice, but Gillian didn't seem to be listening. "She said she took pills from her parents' medicine chest and drank a glass of vodka. She was throwing up in the bathroom. I'm afraid she's really sick."

Dad didn't say anything at first. He just nodded slowly, looking at Gillian with a grave expression. He didn't seem angry at me for bringing her here.

"She said she didn't want to be taken to the nurse's office. She said she was afraid she'd get kicked out of school. Dad, what should I do?"

Gillian was making those shallow, ratchety breathing sounds again, almost as if she was fighting her nausea. While I stood there, frightened, not knowing what to do, Dad placed a trash can by Gillian's feet. He motioned for me to come to Gillian and hold back her hair as she leaned over the trash can. I needed both hands to contain all of her hair. I turned my face away, my nose wrinkling.

Dad opened the door of a little refrigerator he kept in his office and took out a can of ginger ale. He popped it open and placed it on the desk. Then he went to the bathroom and came back with some wet paper towels.

"Wipe her face with these," Dad said, "and try to get her to drink a few sips of ginger ale. I'll be back." He gave me a little smile and squeezed my shoulder, then left the room.

"I feel so awful," Gillian moaned.

"Here." I got down on my knees beside her and offered her the ginger ale. She took maybe two sips, then her hand started shaking and I took the can from her. I wiped her forehead with the cool wet towels, hoping I was making her feel a little bit better. I was too overwhelmed to be thinking much at all, but I couldn't help but feel sorry for her. What could make her, with all of her friends and wealth and popularity, think she had no other choice but to swallow a bunch of pills? As down as I've felt at times over the past few years, that was something I had never considered.

Dad returned with the school nurse, Mrs. Whitley.

"No—" Gillian looked fearful, but the nurse hushed her gently and placed a hand on her forehead.

"Can you tell me what happened?" Mrs. Whitley got on her knees next to Gillian.

Dad motioned for me to follow him out of the room, so I did. He shut the door behind him, and we walked down the hallway and up the stairs to the lobby.

I kept looking back, wondering if I should be in there with Gillian.

Dad must have noticed my expression. "Everything's under control," he said. He led me to a couch in the lobby, and we sat down together.

"What's happening now?"

"The ambulance is on its way," Dad said. "They're going to keep the students in third period until the ambulance leaves so there won't be a commotion. Mr. Gardenhauer's calling her parents right now."

"But that's exactly what Gillian didn't want," I said. "She was afraid she'd get expelled if anyone found her."

"You have to remember, we're talking about what's best for Gillian right now." Dad leaned forward, his elbows on his knees. If I was right, he looked disturbed. "What Gillian did today was her way of crying out for help."

"What kind of help?"

Dad looked sad, like he genuinely felt sorry for Gillian. "Whatever help she needs so that she can develop a sense of self-worth."

I wondered if Gillian even knew Dad existed, if she walked by Dad without speaking to him, like almost everyone else did. It was funny how Dad, who went about his job every day largely unnoticed, probably knew more about the ins and outs of this school than anyone else.

"I wasn't sure if you'd be mad at me for bringing her to your office," I said. "I was afraid she wouldn't come with me if I tried to take her to the nurse."

Dad put an arm around my shoulder and held me close. He hadn't done that in a long time. Then again, I hadn't been close enough to him lately for that even to be possible. "You did the right thing. You realized that the situation was too critical to handle on your own."

Dad was right. Sometimes I act like I don't need my parents, but what would I have done today with Gillian if Dad hadn't been there for me?

Two men pulling a stretcher came through the front doors just then, followed by a woman carrying a large box, and the headmaster, Mr. Gardenhauer, who must have been outside waiting for them. Dad and I turned around to watch as Gillian was brought up the stairs, leaning against the nurse. The ambulance workers took over, leading Gillian to the stretcher, where they lay her down and started wheeling her out. The other person was peering into Gillian's eyes and asking her questions as they left, the nurse trailing after them. All the commotion was over in a few minutes, and Mr. Gardenhauer closed the front doors. His face visibly strained, he turned to Dad and me.

"Thank you, Stephanie," he said to me.

I wasn't sure why he was thanking me when I hadn't really done anything, but I nodded.

"And thank you, Dennis," he said to Dad. "I'm going to keep trying to reach Mr. or Mrs. Sporer." He went into his office and shut the door behind him.

"Her parents don't know yet?" I asked Dad.

Dad looked sad. "Sometimes the parents of these kids can be hard to reach."

"I don't know what to think at all," I said. "It just doesn't sound right to say I feel sorry for Gillian."

"Do you?" Dad asked.

I nodded, and I understood then why most people hated the idea of pity. When it's insincere, it's useless. But even when you mean it, pity is one of the most helpless feelings there is.

The bell rang, fifteen minutes later than it was supposed to, and the large front staircase was soon crowded with students. I remained on the sofa with Dad. It seemed so petty and silly to me now, how I used to try avoiding Dad in the hallway.

"It's lunchtime," Dad said, standing up, "and I'm behind schedule. Are you going to be all right?"

I nodded. "Dad?"

He looked at me, and I faltered. When I remembered the cruel words I'd said to him last night, part of me was surprised that Dad would want to speak to me at all. There was so much

I wanted to say, to apologize for. "Thanks." It seemed inadequate, just that one little word. I should have said so much more.

Dad smiled a little, then continued to the staircase, where he was immediately absorbed into the crowd of students on lunch break.

twenty-one

I wanted to believe that all thoughts of my parents, Miss Winnie, Vance, and now Gillian would fade mercifully as I began the tedious monotony of *pliés* and *tendus* in Madame Caroline's class. No matter how much turmoil swirled around me, ballet class never changed. In the studio, I went to my usual spot at the barre, trying to lose myself in the familiar smells of rosin and sweat, the familiar sound of our accompanist warming up on the piano. I kept looking toward the door, waiting for Vance to come in. He usually took class with us before rehearsal. The rest of the class wandered into the studio in twos and threes. I nodded distractedly when comments were directed my way. I couldn't keep my eyes off the door.

Madame Caroline clapped her hands, signaling the beginning of class. My heart sank. No Vance. The thought of his not dancing still hurt. It seemed like we communicated best when we were dancing, especially at Miss Winnie's house.

As hard as I tried, I really couldn't concentrate on class. Vance may have kissed me last night, but both of us were so torn apart emotionally that it probably didn't mean much. And we went to different schools, had different interests. What reason would we have to see each other? But the thought of his fading out of my life was impossible to bear. And Miss Winnie . . .

During the *petit allegro* combination, I jumped the wrong way and crashed into Anna, both of us tumbling to the floor together. I jumped up and helped her to her feet. "Sorry," I said. Anna shrugged it off and smiled. It was Madame Caroline who gave me a look of icy venom for running into her star pupil.

After class I went to the dressing room to change into pointe shoes, then hung around the lobby, staring up the staircase almost like I could make Vance appear with the power of my mind. He had promised me he would be here!

In the studio, Madame Caroline was directing everyone to their places for the Act 3 wedding scene, where Vance and Anna dance their grand pas de deux. I don't really dance at all in the final scene. I'm just a wedding guest who has to stand through all of the entertainment performed in the Prince and Princess's honor. Then in the final tableau I'm lifted high into the air, where I bless the happy union. I wasn't looking forward to standing around for the next few hours while Madame Caroline rehearsed other people. But all rehearsals involve standing around and waiting as much as they involve dancing.

When I entered the studio, I could tell she was livid. When

Madame Caroline gets really angry, the color drains from her face. "Where is our Prince?" she asked in that low voice that had all of us looking down at our feet.

"He's not here," Camilla said, the only one who dared reply

It was one of the worst rehearsals we'd ever had. Poor Bridget kept making mistakes in her Bluebird dance with Chris and was near tears over Madame Caroline's biting critiques. Anna performed the pas de deux alone, but Madame Caroline told Chris to start learning the role. Everything seemed to be falling apart.

When Mom picked me up after rehearsal, I asked her to take me to Miss Winnie's house.

Mom looked puzzled. "Why do you want to—"

I took deep breaths so I wouldn't snap at her. "Look, a lot of stuff is happening. I'll explain later, but it's important. I'm worried about her."

Mom started the car, but she still wore that puzzled look that told me my words probably weren't making any sense.

"I'll explain later; I will! But if you won't take me, then I'll take a cab!" My voice sounded shrill. I couldn't hide my impatience.

Mom looked hurt, but she agreed to drive me to Miss Winnie's house. "And how long do you plan on staying there?"

"Not long," I remembered what I said last night, and added, "I'm not running away or anything." I turned to Mom and took her free hand in mine for a moment. She glanced at me, surprised, before turning to face the road.

When she pulled up in front of Miss Winnie's house, I said, "I'll be home soon." Then I hurried up the front walk to the house.

The downstairs windows were lit, and I saw a shadow moving behind the opaque draperies in the living room. Someone was home. I rang the doorbell, suddenly nervous.

Vance opened the door. For a moment we looked at each other. He wore jeans, a T-shirt, and a baseball cap. It was hard to picture him in the velvet tunic and tights of a Prince in a classical ballet.

"What's up." If he was surprised to see me, he didn't show it.

"Is Miss Winnie here?" My voice was equally curt.

Vance stepped aside to let me in.

"You said you'd be in rehearsal today."

"Yeah, well, something came up."

I kept my eyes on him until he started shifting uncomfortably on his feet. He looked to the floor. A large duffel bag rested beside the door.

"Where are you going?" I asked.

"A homeboy's. For a while."

"Oh," I said. I wanted to scream at him for missing rehearsal, going back on his promise. I also wanted to kick him in the stomach and watch him crumple to the floor. And part of me wanted to rise to *relevé* on one foot while extending a leg behind me in *arabesque*, reach out and take his hand, and look into his eyes as he promenaded me in a circle. But the weight of all of those feelings in me collapsed into a weird, tired numbness. "Oh" was all I could say.

Miss Winnie wasn't in the living room. For a moment I stared at all of the pretty things: the dolls and the music boxes on the bookcases, the pointe shoes lined in a neat row on the end tables, the black-and-white photographs on the walls of Miss Winnie as a young dancer. The room was so beautiful.

And yet it was almost like a room in a doll's house, too, a place where you could shut out the rest of the world, pretend it didn't exist. There were no mirrors in this room. I had never noticed that before. No mirrors to force you to see yourself as you are, so that you could sit on one of the leather couches, shut your eyes, and be anyone you wanted to be.

I made my way to the kitchen, where Miss Winnie's silver tea service lay gleaming on the table. But she wasn't there, either. Nor was she in the studio, where the moonlight cast a glow on the floor like a spotlight on a darkened stage. I ran my hand along the smooth wooden barre as I walked the length of the studio. How many Sundays had I spent in this room with Miss Winnie and Vance, working, trying, failing, falling, and succeeding? I think those Sundays were some of the happiest times in my life. Who had ever believed in me the way Miss Winnie had? Who had ever listened to my dreams as enthusiastically as she did? But more than that, here at Miss Winnie's house I realized how much I love ballet. When I'm dancing, I'm completely alive. I can do anything.

Closing my eyes, I remembered the night I fled Kelly's party and came here. No, Miss Winnie had said when I asked her if she ever found fulfillment as a professional ballet dancer. There was no place for Miss Winnie in American ballet in the 1940s and 1950s because she was black. Just like there was probably no place in any ballet company today for that wonderful dancer at the SAB audition because she was large. And there was just the tiniest of openings for me. But would that really change the wonderful feeling I get from dancing? Could that ever really change?

Vance was in the room with me. I could feel his presence,

sense his movement. He didn't turn on the lights and both of us stood in the darkness. "So aren't you gonna yell at me for missing rehearsal?"

"You have to do what you have to do." My voice sounded odd, distant, almost as if it wasn't me speaking. My words surprised me, but they also made sense. I remembered the look on Vance's face when he was dancing at that nightclub, playing to the crowd. Maybe club dancing gave him the same kind of pure joy that ballet gave me. How could I argue with that? How could I tell him that was wrong?

"You should call Madame Caroline and tell her you're quitting *Sleeping Beauty.*" I left the studio, left Vance standing there. I had said all I could think of to say. An eerie calmness came over me as I mounted the stairs to find Miss Winnie. It wasn't that I knew what I would say to her. I just felt like I knew something, somewhere deep down inside.

A thin crack of light shone under a closed door at the end of a hallway and I rapped the door softly. "Miss Winnie?"

No answer. I tried the door handle, and it turned easily. The door opened onto a rather large bedroom with a plush armchair positioned by the window. A single antique lamp gave weak light; long shadows formed intricate patterns on the walls and the floor. Miss Winnie sat in the semidarkness, looking out the window.

She looked oddly frail, and then I realized this was the first time I had seen her without a turban or a hat. Her hair was completely gray and gathered loosely at the back of her neck. She wore a thin blue dressing gown, and her hands were folded into her lap. She looked so old to me. I had never really thought of her as old before. But without her elaborate gowns and turbans, in a simple blue nightdress, she looked almost like a different person.

She didn't notice me come in. Her lips trembled slightly, and her cheeks were glazed with tears.

"Miss Winnie?" I hurried over to her, wanting to throw my arms around her neck, wanting to tell her how much she meant to me, anything to make her smile, to bring the look of joy to her face that I knew so well. I placed my hands over hers and squeezed them gently, just as Vance had done to me last night.

It seemed like Miss Winnie attempted a smile, but it fell from her face, and her head drooped slightly.

"I've been wanting to see you since last night."

She lifted her head slightly, looking into my eyes. "He's leaving me." Her eyes brimmed over with tears.

I squeezed her hands again, feeling hot tears on my own face. You'll have me, I thought I would exclaim, but I didn't say that. "He'll never leave you," I said. "He loves you so much." Although Vance had never said that to me, I knew with everything in me that it was true.

"But what did I do wrong?" Miss Winnie's voice grew fainter, and I knew she was talking to herself more than she was talking to me. "What did I do wrong to make him turn away from me?"

"Vance, he wants something different, that's all. I love dancing with Vance. It makes me sad to think he doesn't love ballet as much as I do. But . . ." I stopped speaking and put my arms around Miss Winnie's neck, smelled the familiar spicy-sweet scent that infused her skin.

"All I wanted was the best for him," she said, "and the best for you, too."

"You believed in Vance and me so much that we figured out how to believe in ourselves. And once Vance did that, he realized what it was that he really loves. And now he has to go after his dream, just like I have to go after mine."

Miss Winnie looked at me, almost as if she wasn't quite understanding me.

I smiled at her. "I would have loved to see you dance. I would have loved to sit in that audience in Germany or in New York and watch you. Because you know what dancing is all about. It's not about how many *pirouettes* you can do or how high you can lift your legs. It's about loving what you do and wanting to show the world how much you love it. That's what you taught me. And no one can ever take that away from me, whether I make it as a ballerina or not. Just like no one could take that away from you."

Miss Winnie looked at me. "You'll be going to the San Francisco Ballet School audition tomorrow, right?" Her eyes were so full of hope and eagerness as she awaited my answer.

"Yes, I'm going," I said after a moment, "but I have to start being realistic about my future, too."

Miss Winnie looked puzzled.

"What if I get a serious injury? Or what if I don't get asked to join any ballet companies? If I feel like I'll die if I don't make it as a ballet dancer, then I'll be dancing because I'm afraid to fail, not because it's what I love to do."

Miss Winnie sat still for a moment. "I always thought, maybe I didn't have the opportunity, but I could give that opportunity to my nephew, to you—"

"You have," I said. "You have."

The door squeaked, and I turned around to see Vance peering in at us. I had no idea how long he had been standing there.

Miss Winnie looked up when she saw him. She wiped her

eyes with her sleeve. "Will you be leaving soon?" Her voice was formal, barely masking her sadness.

His shoulders went up and down, and he stared at the floor. "I guess I can stick around."

I saw the relief in Miss Winnie's face, and I wiped my eyes quickly. "Um, I need to be getting home."

"I'll take you," Vance said without raising his eyes from the floor.

I turned to Miss Winnie. "You'll be all right?"

She nodded. "Tell me how the audition goes tomorrow?"

"I will."

She hesitated before speaking again. "Maybe we can have class on Sunday?"

I hugged her again. "Of course. I'll be here."

Miss Winnie smiled then. I kissed her cheek and said goodbye.

Vance didn't speak to me until we were in the car and he had turned the ignition.

"What made you decide to stay?" I asked Vance once we were in the car.

Vance didn't answer for a long time. When he did, he said, "She's been good to me."

"Are you going to call Madame Caroline?"

"I don't know. It's not that I don't like it, I just—" He sighed, sounding frustrated.

"It's just not what you want to do."

"That's not what I meant," Vance said. "I don't know, I guess I said I'd drop out of the ballet to get back at Miss Winnie more than anything else."

"What are you saying?"

"It'd suck for me to just drop out now."

My breath caught in my throat. "So you're staying in *Sleeping Beauty*?"

He shrugged and nodded.

"And then—"

"Me and Corey and James, we're gonna try to make a go of this club thing," Vance said. "There's a big dance competition in Los Angeles in June. We're gonna try to go."

I nodded. I'm sure my disappointment showed on my face. But I tried to make my voice light. "I'm glad you're not backing out of *Sleeping Beauty*."

Now Vance smiled a little. "I said I wouldn't, didn't I?"

"I guess so."

He leaned close to me, but instead of kissing me, he put his arms around my waist and held me close. I rested my head on his shoulder, and we didn't need to talk. I felt the warmth of his neck, the softness of his shirt against my cheek. Whatever happened next, I knew we were not going to drift apart. And that was all I needed to know right now.

twenty-two

Just as I had expected, the whole school was talking about what had happened with Gillian the day before. Even though the students had been kept in their classes until the ambulance left, Gillian's situation became common knowledge minutes after the bell rang.

During study hall I lay my head on my desk, exhausted but clear-headed. The San Francisco Ballet School audition was after school today, but I wasn't anticipating it nervously, or even thinking about it. It just wasn't all that important in the grand scheme of things, any more than not getting the lead in *Sleeping Beauty.* It wasn't that I would never worry about auditions or casting ever again. Those things wouldn't be life or death for me. Not now.

I was surprised when Kelly and Lisa came to sit next to me.

I smelled them before I saw them: the hairspray, chewing gum, perfume, cigarette smoke. Both of them were somber in a way I had never seen them look before. I felt my guard rising anyway, because they never spoke to me unless they wanted something from me.

"Have you talked to Gillian since yesterday?" Lisa spoke first, leaning toward me.

I shook my head. "Do you know what happened to her?"

"She got her stomach pumped and now she's at home," Lisa said. "I talked to her mom last night. Gillian wouldn't talk to me."

Kelly looked distraught. "To either of us."

"Her mom said she's gonna be out of school for a while. She might not come back this year at all," Lisa said. "Do you know what happened?"

"I found her in the bathroom—"

"I knew there was something weird about her yesterday." Kelly was near tears. "I saw her after first period and all she would say is 'I'm sick of everything. I'm so sick of it!' I thought it might be that new guy she was dating—"

"Frankie?"

"That guy is such a jerk!" Kelly said. "We kept trying and trying to tell her that, hoping she wouldn't get hurt. But I don't think that's all of it. She just seemed so, I don't know . . ."

"She didn't say much. She was really sick."

"But now she won't talk to us!" Kelly started crying now. "We went to her house after school yesterday with flowers, balloons, but her mom said she didn't want to see us."

Lisa grew teary-eyed, too. "I don't know, maybe she'll talk to you."

"But why me?" I asked. "It's not like we're all that good of friends."

"She really likes you, though," Kelly said.

Really liked me? If that was the truth, Gillian had a weird way of showing it.

"Can you maybe talk to her?" Lisa asked. "Tell her we care about her?"

"What makes you think she'll talk to me?"

"I don't know," Lisa said in a small voice. "But if you could just try. It would mean so much to me—"

"Me, too," Kelly said.

I looked from one to the other as they both dabbed their faces with Kleenex. I never thought either one of them had a compassionate bone in her body. Now I didn't know what to think of them at all. "I'll try," was all I could say. "I can try to see her after school."

Kelly smiled at me, and Lisa told me to call her tonight. She scribbled her number on a piece of paper. "Thanks," she said. "You're the best."

This time, it sounded like she really meant it.

After study hall, I wandered through the hallway, amid a sea of blue uniforms. My eyes traced the dark wood paneling on the walls. The dark blue carpet was nearly spotless. I stood at the top of the large staircase, looking down at the marbled entryway, which sparkled and gleamed under the crystal chandelier. I remembered how parents of new students marveled as they walked into the entryway, how the headmaster led them down the halls with a look of pride on his face. And Dad was the one responsible for it all. He worked hard, arriving early every morning, staying late after classes ended. Maybe he was practically invisible to the students as he walked through the halls, but he did his job well, and he did it with pride. I don't think I ever noticed how beautiful the school looked before today.

Dad took me to see Gillian after school.

"Don't you have ballet class?" he asked me.

"It's canceled today. There's an audition for the San Francisco Ballet School tonight."

"When do you find out if you've gotten accepted at any of these ballet schools?"

"Soon, I hope."

"Do you think you have a chance of being accepted?" Dad asked.

"I have a chance," I said, "but there's no way to predict." And I explained to him how these ballet schools held auditions all over the country, picking the best of the best for their summer programs. A lucky few would be invited to continue on during the year, which gave those few a better chance of getting invited to join the company. Dad listened, nodding with interest.

If Kelly's house was a mansion, Gillian's was a palace. It stood on a hill by itself, the house seeming to look down on all the mansions beneath it as if they were mere cottages. It had a large columned entryway and heavy double doors. Gillian's Mercedes was parked in the driveway, in front of a four-car garage.

"Goodness gracious," Dad said mildly.

I said nothing. I was awestruck.

I had no idea if Gillian would agree to see me at all. She had been sleeping when I called her house at lunchtime, but her mother suggested I come by after school. Standing at the door, I wished I'd brought some flowers or something.

Mrs. Sporer answered the door herself, and I knew she was the lady of the house from her stick-thin figure swathed in designer clothes and the heavy diamond on her left hand. She looked a lot like Gillian, with the same light complexion and curly black hair.

"I'm so glad to see you." She pressed my hand like we were close friends, which made me even more uncomfortable. "Gillian's looking forward to your visit."

The foyer looked more like a museum than a home. I had never seen anything like it. There was even a waterfall trickling along a back wall. It was the kind of place where I'd feel afraid to touch anything, to sit on the chairs.

Mrs. Sporer led me up a staircase and down a long hallway. She opened the door onto a large, airy room practically the size of the whole downstairs area of my house. It was nothing at all like I expected. The bed had a frilly coverlet, with matching drapes. The furniture was white, with gold trim. It looked like a little girl's room.

Gillian was sitting up in bed with a book lying open beside her. She looked wan and listless, her hair lying in limp strings against her pillow. Without makeup she looked young and almost plain. She didn't smile, but her eyes lit up when she saw me. Mrs. Sporer left the room, closing the door behind her.

"I guess you never thought you'd see me like this," Gillian said. "Have a seat." She patted the bed, and I perched on the edge.

"How are you?"

She shrugged. "I really want a smoke, but Mom took away all my cigarettes. Got one?"

"I don't smoke. You know that."

"Oh yeah, you're probably not allowed. With ballet and everything." She wore her usual bored-casual look, which I immediately found annoying. There was no point in pretending everything was okay when it so obviously wasn't.

"Lisa and Kelly are worried about you," I said.

Gillian laughed a little. "I'll bet."

"They said they came to see you yesterday, but you wouldn't see them. They both asked me today during study hall to come talk to you."

Gillian looked like she didn't care. "My parents say they're gonna send me to this boarding school in New Mexico. That'll be my fourth high school. Maybe I'll go for a record!"

I've felt all kinds of conflicting emotions around Gillian. I've felt intimidated, annoyed, angry, jealous, admiring, confused, and frustrated. But now all I felt for her was pity. I really didn't have any idea who this girl was. And I don't think she had any idea, either.

"So everybody's talking about me, right?" she said. "But so what? I'll be old news on Monday." Her face crumpled suddenly and she lowered her head. She wiped her eyes with both hands. That bored-casual look returned.

"So how's ballet going, anyway?" She sounded snide. "And what about that guy you dance with? Is there anything going on between you? Or wait a minute, I'll bet he's gay!"

"Why do you have to be so mean?"

That was not what she was expecting me to say. Gillian looked at me suspiciously.

"I'm not being mean," she said, as if I had annoyed her. "I just call things as I see them."

"I don't even think you like me."

Gillian fell silent. She glared at me, almost outraged.

"It's like you want to be my friend, you're nice to me, then you go out of your way to make me uncomfortable."

"You should lighten up. You take everything too seriously." Gillian sounded really annoyed now.

I didn't say anything.

"I don't know, I thought you'd be cool to hang out with sometimes. But all you care about is ballet. I just thought I'd try to help you have a social life. I felt sorry for you."

I almost laughed at that. Maybe I would have bought that a few months ago, but there was no way I'd buy that now. I stood up. It didn't look as if we really had anything to say to each other. "Well, I just thought I'd come by and see how you were doing. I guess you're back to your old self."

I turned toward the door and Gillian said, "Wait!"

I turned around again and that bored, smug expression was replaced with a look of desperation. She was breathing heavily.

"Don't go," she said.

"I have an audition to get to."

"Well, can you just wait a few minutes?" She looked like she was near tears. So I went back to her bed and sat down.

Gillian lowered her head, and it took me a moment to realize she was crying.

"Gillian?"

"I'm just so sick of all this." She looked up and I thought I was really seeing her for the first time. She looked small and unsure of herself. She looked the way I've so often felt walking through the halls at school. But there was something else, too, a deeper pain that she probably didn't know how to express.

"What?" I said, nodding to tell her to go on.

A few tears seeped out of her eyes. "I'm sick of trying to fit in everywhere, to say the right thing, to wear the right thing. Sometimes I don't even feel like I'm me. It's like some fake Gillian lives inside my body and she's the girl who's cool, and me, I don't even know . . ."

She turned to me, glaring at me, it seemed like. "You can't know what I'm talking about! You have your ballet, and that's what makes you special. But me, take away my car and my clothes and my allowance, and what's left?" She stopped for a moment, as if she was considering the possibility. "I've always had this fantasy of going to a big public school, driving a Ford or something. But then I'd just be nobody."

"That's not true."

"I used to think that was it, you know? Go to public school where there're more black kids. But I don't really fit in with Frankie and Clay and his friends any more than I fit in here."

"But what about Lisa and Kelly and Bret, you fit in with them—"

Gillian shut her eyes and shook her head, frustrated. "How can I fit in when I don't even know who I am? I catch myself talking sometimes and I think, Gillian, you are such a bitch! But it's just easier to be that way, to play along. But I'm sick of it. I'm just so sick of it. . . ."

She looked at me and gave a tiny smile. "When I first got here, I was hoping so much that we could be friends. I don't know, I guess I messed everything up." She sounded disgusted. "I guess that's what I'm really good at. I'll bet Lisa and Kelly hate me now."

"No, they don't," I said softly.

"Frankie does," she muttered. "I went over to his house the day before yesterday and went up to his room. He was on the phone, and he didn't hear me behind the door. He was talking about me on the phone, talking about how easy I was and what a bore I was."

I winced at that, feeling deeply sorry for her.

She shrugged, and that bored look returned. "I guess he's right, isn't he? I mean, what am I good for? All I ever do is mess things up!" She lowered her head and started crying again. I sat with her for a few moments.

"Maybe we can do something together soon," I said tentatively.

She looked up. "You mean it?"

"Sure. As soon as you're feeling better."

She smiled though her tears. "Thank you."

I looked at my watch. "Um, I have to be going. . . ." I was glad I had the audition to get me out of there. It was the same feeling I'd had yesterday, that her problems were too big for me to take on by myself. Maybe I could be her friend, but I couldn't help her solve her problems.

She looked genuinely disappointed, but she nodded.

On the way to the audition, all I could think about was Gillian. Not what happened yesterday—that was too much to deal with, but everything she had said about not knowing who she was. I understood that, more than I realized. How many times had I looked forward to ballet class as a way to avoid thinking about my life, the things that bothered me, school? Ballet is great and it's terrible that way. It's so consuming that you can spend all your time thinking about nothing else, all the while your problems festering inside you. It was weird and ironic, how all of us in Madame Caroline's class looked to ballet for security when ballet had no real security to offer.

At the Colorado Ballet Academy, I was thankful for the opportunity to put all of my swirling thoughts and emotions out of my head and concentrate on performing dance steps as proficiently as I could. But there was another feeling there that I didn't even notice until I caught my reflection in the mirror during the *grand allegro.* I was happy just to be dancing.

twenty-three

The next few weeks whizzed by in a flurry of technical rehearsals, costume fittings, and dress rehearsals; before I knew it, it was opening night of *The Sleeping Beauty.* I woke up at noon that Saturday with frazzled nerves. Dress rehearsal the night before had not gone well. Vance missed an entrance, and the younger girls in the corps de ballet couldn't do anything right. But people always say bad dress rehearsals mean good performances.

Yesterday was also a bad day because I found out I had been rejected by both the Pacific Northwest Ballet School summer program and the San Francisco Ballet School. The Pacific Northwest rejection was no surprise; no one had looked at me at that audition, but I had felt good about San Francisco. I thought the judges were really watching me. I couldn't help but feel jealous as Madame Caroline congratulated Anna on getting accepted at Pacific Northwest, San Francisco, and the School of American Ballet before class yesterday. I hadn't heard from SAB yet, but I figured if I hadn't heard by now, then I must not have gotten in. Vance had been accepted, with full scholarship, at Pacific Northwest, but when I asked him if there was any chance of his going, he shook his head with an emphatic no. He'd been rejected at SAB, but as badly as he'd danced at the audition, that was no surprise.

But I couldn't think about that today. I had to put all of my energy into dancing well tonight in *Sleeping Beauty.* Maybe I wasn't the star, but I could still show the audience what I could do. I went upstairs to eat something, and both of my parents were in the kitchen, smiling at me.

"Good afternoon, sleepyhead!" Dad said.

"What?" I said, irritable. Dress rehearsal had run late last night, and I was still sore and tired.

"Look on the table," Mom said.

Two opened pieces of mail with my name on them lay on the kitchen table. I bristled at that. The first was a catalog from Stanford.

"Read the letter," Dad said. I picked up the letter and skimmed quickly. It sounded the same as the other college letters I'd gotten. "We were impressed with your PSAT scores—" I set it down without finishing it. I suppose it should have made me happy, but it didn't. I guessed I was really going to have to start thinking about college.

"Did you read it?" Mom asked.

I poured myself some orange juice. "It's great." I sounded pretty unenthusiastic.

"Did you read both letters?" Dad said in a teasing voice. "There were two letters in the catalog."

Growing annoyed, I shook the catalog until it fell open to a section on the Fine Arts program. A single sheet of paper fluttered out of it and my eyes immediately zoned in on the letterhead: The School of American Ballet.

"You opened it?" I shrieked, furious. I snatched the paper and began skimming it quickly. "Dear Stephanie, We're happy to offer you a place in our summer program—"

I couldn't read any further. I think I screamed out loud. Then I started jumping up and down. Mom and Dad sat at the table, smiling. I hardly knew what I was saying. It must have been something like "I got in! I got in!"

"Hold on, hold on," Dad said. "Read the rest of it."

Not only had I gotten in, I'd been given a scholarship. My eyes scanned the page two, three times to make sure I was reading it correctly.

"Oh my goodness—" I didn't know what to say. I think I was crying.

"We can handle your airfare and spending money," Dad said. "Congratulations."

I flew into his arms then. Then I hugged Mom. "I can't believe it. This is so amazing."

My parents couldn't stop smiling. They seemed truly excited for me, not worried, not annoyed.

"I'm going to New York!" I began jumping up and down again. I was going to study at the school that produced Darci Kistler and Suzanne Farrell and Merrill Ashley, the school where Miss Winnie took classes taught by George Balanchine.

But then I sat down as reality surfaced. I was still excited and still on cloud nine, but I couldn't ignore reality. Yes, I was invited to the summer program. I'd made the cut. But that wasn't a guarantee of anything. What if all the dancers were better than me? What if no one paid any attention to me? The chances were slim, even in the best of circumstances, that I would be one of the lucky few asked to stay on at the end of the summer.

"What is it?" Mom asked.

"I'll start looking at the college catalogs tomorrow," I said. "I know there aren't any guarantees that they'll ask me to stay."

My parents didn't say anything, but they nodded. If I was correct, Dad looked proud.

At the theater before the performance, everyone in my class buzzed around me, excited for me. Madame Caroline even gave me a warm "congratulations." I guess Anna and I were the only ones accepted into SAB. Bridget was put on the waiting list at Boston and Houston. Camilla and Ursula would be spending the summer at their grandparents' farm in New Hampshire.

"Who wants to spend all summer dancing?" Camilla said with a smile. She and Ursula both hugged me, happy for me. We were all in the dressing room, putting on the thick, heavy makeup needed for the stage. My lavender tutu hung on the costume rack. I leaned toward the mirror, carefully applying black eyeliner. Anna, who didn't enter until after the Prologue, stretched on the floor in a leotard and tights.

"I heard you got acceptance at SAB," she said to me. "Congratulations."

I smiled. "So we'll be going together." How wonderful it would be to go to New York with a familiar face.

Anna looked somber. She had already put on her makeup, streaks of pink and red and white that would make her look stunning on stage, even if she looked like a sorceress right now. "I don't know. Maybe I cannot. It's very expensive—"

"Didn't you get a scholarship?"

"But there is the airplane ticket—"

"I'm sure you can get a special fare or something."

Anna shook her head. "My parents, they run a motel. Sometimes I must work there. I'm not sure I can be away the whole summer."

"There has to be a way," I said firmly. "There just has to be."

Anna smiled, but she didn't look very optimistic. "I hope we can go together, too."

The stage manager gave the fifteen-minute call, and I hurried into my costume. At Gillian's house last week, she had helped me come up with a new hairdo: a series of cornrows twisting up into a crown on top of my head. It looked regal and beautiful. Anna zipped me into my costume, and I dabbed my face with a Kleenex. I was ready to dance.

I stood in the wings, testing my pointe shoes and taking deep breaths as the overture began. When the music started, all of my nerves melted away. I was going to enjoy this, enjoy doing what I loved best on the stage. Chris met me in the back wing, majestic-looking in his tunic and tights.

"Ready?" he said with a wink. He lifted me up and on cue, carried me onto the stage, into the world of *Sleeping Beauty.*

During the Prologue I was the star, getting a burst of applause after my solo variation. Then Anna took command of the ballet during Act 1. She was beautiful in the Rose Adagio, a dance with four men in which she got applause for the wonderfully difficult balances. In the Act 2 vision scene, she and Vance were amazing. For all of Vance's ambivalence about ballet, when he was on stage, he was as charismatic as he was at the club that time. He was a born performer.

Act 3 was the most uncomfortable for me, because I had to stand in character through all of the wedding dances. Standing on stage is so much harder than dancing. I had to keep sending messages to my standing leg, rocking on it ever so slightly so it wouldn't go to sleep.

The dances culminated in the grand pas de deux, the final showpiece for Anna and Vance. It started well enough, full of incredible leaps, balances, supported turns, and lifts. But during the end of the coda, Anna slipped as she glided toward Vance and went crashing to the stage. I heard a collective gasp from the audience, but she was up on her feet quickly and finished the dance without further mishap.

I could see Anna's chest heaving through the finale and after the ballet was over, after all of the applause and ovations, she went backstage and burst into tears.

All of us stood around her, the younger girls trying to tell her how great she was, how the little stumble didn't matter. Then I saw a flash of gold out of the corner of my eye. I turned around and saw Miss Winnie, who had made her way backstage.

She looked as splendid as always in her gold turban and gold dress. I wanted to run to her, tell her my news about the School of American Ballet. She smiled at me, but then I saw her eyes shift to Anna. Her face was full of compassion. She went straight to Anna and put a comforting arm around her shoulder.

"Do not be afraid of falling, dear," I heard Miss Winnie saying. "I remember seeing Suzanne Farrell fall on stage once—it's better to fall attempting something wonderful than to hold back. . . ."

I separated myself from the crowd and wandered back onto the stage. Vance was standing there, looking out as if he could see the auditorium through the closed curtain. I wondered what he was doing there. The stagehands moved around him, taking down the scenery from Act 3 and putting up the Prologue scene for tomorrow's performance.

I walked over to him. "What's going on?"

"You were really good," he said to me.

"So were you."

He slung an arm around my shoulder, and I pressed my cheek against the soft velvet of his tunic.

"Will it be hard to give all of this up?"

Vance shrugged. "It was fun while it lasted."

"Just think. If you had done better at the SAB audition, you could have gone to New York with me."

He laughed at that. "But who says I need to go to SAB to go to New York? They've got some dance contests there, too."

"So you might come?"

He squeezed my shoulders. "Maybe."

In the wings, my parents waited for me, dressed in their Sunday best. Dad held a huge bouquet of red roses. I smiled at them, and they smiled back, nodding as if they understood I would be out to see them soon.

Gillian was in the wings, too, dressed in one of her snazzy black outfits. I was surprised to see Lisa and Kelly with her, too. I smiled back at them, too, but I wasn't ready to walk off stage just yet. Sure, we had another performance tomorrow, but there was something final about this night. I'm not sure what it was.

Out of nowhere, it seemed like, Vance extended his arm to

me. I took his hand, not understanding what he was doing until I heard him humming the balcony theme from *Romeo and Juliet* under his breath. Miss Winnie's pas de deux, the one she made for us. I rose to pointe and we began to dance, both of us humming off-key. And it felt right, to be dancing behind the closed curtain, stagehands wandering around behind us, the wings crammed with audience members, both of us dressed in our *Sleeping Beauty* costumes. I could almost imagine us on a moonlit night in Verona, professing our love as Romeo and Juliet. But the image of the balcony in Verona soon faded until I realized I was really seeing Miss Winnie's studio, Vance and me dancing together in the darkness. I could feel Miss Winnie's presence in the front wing, and I knew she was watching us. I leaped toward Vance and soon he was holding me high in the air over his head. The air up there felt wonderful, pure, unpolluted. I held my balance as he walked me in a slow circle around the stage, both of us singing the music, only two hands on my hipbones providing my support. But I felt as secure over Vance's head as I've felt anywhere. He lowered me gently and looked into my eyes. I was conscious of the incredible feeling I had, dancing with Vance on stage with my friends and family in the wings, and most of all, the soft applause and the shining eyes of Miss Winnie, standing in that front wing.

Lorri Hewett, a 1994 graduate of Emory College, completed the manuscripts for nine novels before she graduated from high school, and published her first book as a senior. Since then she has published *Lives of Our Own* (Dutton and Puffin) and *Soulfire* (Dutton and Puffin). She lives in Decatur, Georgia.